Set My Heart in Aspic

Nisha Da Cunha was born in 1934. She went to school in Simla and Delhi. She studied English Literature at Miranda House, New Delhi before going on to Cambridge, U.K. for post-graduate studies. She taught English Literature at Miranda House for five years and then for twenty-five years pursued an extremely successful teaching career at St. Xavier's College, Mumbai, from where she resigned as Head of the Department in 1985. Nisha has directed several plays, including Carson McCuller's *Member of the Wedding* and Ibsen's *The Wild Duck*. Two of her earlier works are *Old Cypress* (1991) and *The Permanence of Grief* (1993). In 1996, a film based on her story *Three Lives* was screened at NCPA.

Nisha Da Cunha is married with one son and lives in Mumbai.

Praise for Nisha Da Cunha

There is a sadness which is quite unsentimental and is linked up with some of the great tragic themes of western literature.

David Daiches

The work is uncomfortable, disturbing reading, but by the same token once read it lingers on in the corridors of the mind, its emotional impact, intact long after the superstructure, the narrative, the characters have dimmed in one's memory.

Financial Express

There is a finely-crafted feel to all the long passages that suggests thoughtful consideration rather than a hysterical spontaneity.

The Independent

The sensibility is entirely feminine, and sometimes reminiscent of Katherine Manefield — the perceptions are made with the clarity of mind that sometimes comes to an invalid, a sharpening of the senses through a knowledge of pain, the world seen through withdrawal.

India Today

Set My Heart in Aspic

Nisha Da Cunha

HarperCollins *Publishers* India

All the events and people in these stories are fictional
All the landscapes are real.

HarperCollins *Publishers* India Pvt Ltd
7/16 Ansari Road, Daryaganj, New Delhi 110 002

First published 1997 by
HarperCollins *Publishers* India
Second edition 1999

Nisha Da Cunha asserts the moral right
to be identified as the author of this work

ISBN 81-7223-283-7

Typeset by
Megatechnics
19A, Ansari Road
New Delhi 110 002

Printed in India by
Gopsons Papers Ltd
A-14 Sector 60
Noida 201 301

For
Rahul and Radhika
and
in memory of
Ginger
1979-1994

Contents

Quotations'
Acknowledgements

Golden Beach Boys: Old Testament

The Girl in a Burkha, Riding a Cycle: William Golding,
   W.B. Yeats

Books Last: Ntozake Shange

Set My Heart in Aspic: Old Testament, Shakespeare

Wintersmoke: Rilke, W.H. Auden

Le Loire Noire: Jane Kenyon

Ithaka: C.P. Cavafy, Gerald Manley Hopkins

1 *Something Old, Something New*

Something old,
Something new,
Something borrowed,
Something blue.

That's how the old rhyme went and Bird wanted it to be like that for herself. God knows she had waited long enough. It was old fashioned but that's what she liked the best.

The Victorians in period, old paintings, old-fashioned clothes. She did not of course give the appearance of being like that. She seemed always trendy and quaint in the way she dressed and cut her hair and her taste in music, the way she danced, in everything. She was very tiny, a sparrow. She was nicknamed Bird. She planned to be married before she was forty. And did. Just.

But just. All her life she had been made to adjust and she said with great determination — "once I am married, no more adjustments. Absolutely not. I'll not adjust anymore. Life is going to be very different. Things will go my way. Other people can adjust. For a change. I seem to have spent more than half of my life adjusting — it could easily go on for the rest of it. I'll not let that happen."

On her wedding morning her wisdom tooth came out. Deathly scared of dentists she bore great pain for over a fortnight and then it came out, "just in time; I could not have borne it another day. Like a miracle the pain is gone. Well, that's luck for me, though now I hope my remaining tooth brings me all I am going to need — in the way of wisdom, I mean."

She felt great freedom, a whole ten days' leave from her school, she taught English (Language-Literature) and felt like a favourite heroine Elizabeth, marrying as she must, her Darcy, Jane, her Rochester. Her sister would be her best woman and she hadn't told her mum yet and her father, she did not dare to tell just in case he stopped everything, as he always did, always had all her life, a great spoiler of fun. She liked him only because he was like all the more tyrannical of Victorian fathers. "I hate him and will never forgive him. Poor Mum, but she's given in all her life and so now she has only his bullying left to show for her whole life." Tomorrow she would be out of this bare, greasy, dirty hostel, away from the geyser that never worked, its filthy discoloured plastic buckets and mugs. Its smell. Its miserable breakfasts. Thinking of breakfasts she thought of the brilliant idea she had had for her wedding. There was to be a breakfast after the ceremony, not the nasty two-hard-fried-eggs-swimming-in-old-oil and two "slices" of stale Britannia bread, but a lavish unusual meal at Woodlands, decorated of course. Innovative, unusual, memorable, also the cheapest of the three meals, and no liquor. Well-read little Bird remembered how in Mary McCarthy's *The Group,* the wedding ended with a breakfast that ended with a baked Alaska. She had always remembered that. So would hers be.

Remembered. Woodlands at ten, six of their friends, three girls from the hostel, tired, nine-to-five grey girls, with two and a half hours of commuting, besides. The restaurant had done them proud with buntings from last Christmas and "happy wedding couple" signs in green and blue everywhere. The dosas and idlis were piping hot, the coffee was real and the cake everyone's favourite. Chocolate.

They left for Goa for a week's holiday. A friend had lent them their old ancestral home for their honeymoon. It was not a total disaster. The lights fused every time they switched on the geyser and K hurt his back climbing onto the four poster bed. But as Bird went to sleep she couldn't help feeling how it couldn't be more fitting. "I've always dreamed of a four-poster bed and this one is more than a century old. I'm like Jane, I'm like Elizabeth, I'm like Dorothea. So my something old is this blessed four-poster bed, my something new is the mosquito coil unwinding under the bed leaving little grey slugs, my something borrowed is my sister's lacy nightie and my something blue, K's pyjamas. So that's all right," she thought and went to sleep.

They got candles the next day and stuff to rub on K's back and discovered that Bird liked gin and K liked rum, Bird liked tea and K liked coffee. K is Gujarati and I am a pale Parsi. K likes Ed McBain, and I love *Middlemarch*. "So what!" thought Bird, "so what!"

The following nights remained uncomfortable not romantic, though they left lots of candles burning all night. The light created odd shadows on the high ceilings and in the shadowed mirrors of the cupboards. But it was an unusual house with its shell-shuttered windows and portraits and old, carved furniture. During the day the sun shone brightly and they hired bicycles and wandered about and ate prawns and chocolate brownies at St. Anthony's. On one of their wanderings they came across an advertisement, it was for a cruise called Crocodile Feast and they decided to go on it. Our adventure. We've seen the sea of Goa and now we will know one of its rivers, an adventure before we go back to grey old Bombay, commuting and grumbling; this will be our adventure before real life and its grind begins.

It was nobody's fault. It was an accident. It wasn't meant to turn out the way it did. The three thin Goa newspapers were full of it for the next week. Nobody could have anticipated any such thing, these cruises were very popular. People had been taken on them for ever such a long time. It was just one of those things. I got most of this from K when he came back, and when I could get him to speak about it all. He was grey and miserable with a sad stubble on his chin.

They had arrived at the meeting place and there were all the other cruise adventurers ready with sun caps and swimming gear and little bags full of this and that, that they might need for the all-day cruise down the river to look at the crocodiles. K said "we took our swimming gear along even though Bird couldn't swim. But she loved the way she looked in her new two-piece costume and a book to read like she always did, you know how Bird was always carrying a book with her wherever she went. 'For all kinds of eventualities' she used to say. The others were rather a nice group of people from all over the world really. One couple, a tall white man who could have been a former colonial Governor and his immensely handsome dark West Indian wife. A charming couple from Leeds who made Puffa jackets for riding, 'even the Royal family wear them', they told us. A few honeymoon couples very wrapped up in each other and Bird and me." The incident was talked about for years after. The couple from Leeds repeated it when anyone asked them about their holidays in India. They always began, "Oh, it was a wonderful holiday except for one very mysterious thing that happened in our last week in Goa. It was on a river trip amusingly called 'Crocodile Feast'. There was this charming honeymoon couple from Bombay, a tiny slip of a girl like a bright bird and her husband. Well the girl disappeared. She really did. It seemed one moment she was with us and a bit later she was nowhere. Not a trace of her. Not a sound, not a splash, nothing. We could hardly get the husband to come back from there to the mainland. Oh, it was terrible, he was inconsolable. He went back with the river patrol, and the police with flares, they searched and searched the whole night and the better part of the next day. Not a trace, poor boy, the poor boy, he took it so bad. So bad. My migraine returned and stayed. I didn't fancy the sun any more, I shall never go back to India."

Another couple said, "We always follow the sun, it's quite simple; we just told the travel agent, we want the sun everyday every waking moment, and they sent us to Goa. Never again."

And it had started out so well. A clear day and a beautiful sky, the sun sparkled on the waves, and everyone sitting on the hard seats of the country craft felt happy, expectant, adventurous ... After nearly two hours on the open sea they entered the mouth of the river, and then

into one of the smaller tributaries and our boat switched
off the outboard motor and suddenly it was very quiet.
All the people spoke in hushed voices. The waters were
very dull, and now no sun filtered through the trees.
Everything turned mysterious and rather menacing. A
jolly fellow started a story but soon stopped, there was
such a feeling of unease. Every log, every green, slimy
branch or tin or scrap of rag seemed filled with fear and
something evil. Someone said, "Look out for crocs."
Someone said "I hope it is just crocs and nothing worse."
Not even a tiny breeze stirred. Only a sudden half-crazed
sound of a bird, lonely, haunted, haunting. Everyone
shivered though it was a warm day. After a fearful hour
they moved into wider waters and a kind of farmhouse
in a clearing where they were to have their lunch.
Suddenly the sun shone again and everyone cheered up
and the beer, the good food helped everyone to forget the
last hour. After the welcome break they all piled back into
the boat and carried on, they spotted two crocodiles, so
that part of things was a success. And then it was time
to start back. It was then they discovered that Bird was
missing. Bird was never found.

2 A Delicate Life

Guy came out to India in 1930. He was twenty-three years young. He was glad to get away from England and his home. He felt suffocated living with his mother. He loved her very much but he needed to get away. He had lived all his life in Bath almost always alone with his mother. His father had died when Guy was a little boy and he had no brothers or sisters. They had all died as infants. Guy grew up a very quiet person who read a great deal and went for long, solitary walks. He had hated school and college. His mother had not allowed him to cut his hair, so he was teased mercilessly in school. Because of his love of reading he found a job in publishing greatly to his taste and worked very hard and very well. There was nothing he did not know about books and what goes into bringing out a well-published book.

He was shy with women and delicate in his ways. He treated all women as he would his mother. When his publishers decided to send him to India he was overjoyed even though it would mean leaving his mother alone.

He was allotted a flat on a hill and he walked to work everyday and back again. It was a considerable distance but he loved the walk. He played chess and became very good at it. It did not involve talking. This pleased him. On the weekends he went walking. He brought maps of the great hills surrounding Bombay and these long, serious walks were his great love. He had a well-trained male servant. He wrote to his mother every Friday evening. For her he also kept a scrapbook with photographs carefully mounted and marked. Little arrows showing height and where he was standing and so on. On hearing that his mother was very ill he went back to Bath and looked after her till she died. He found a grave for her next to his father's.

He was sad to think that his mother would not see the neat historical scrap book he was making for her but he wound up her affairs and sold all the things not needed any more. He sold his house and took back with him only his mother's jewellery box and two needle-point cushion covers that he knew she had been meaning to send to him. On the journey by P & O boat he often looked at the contents of the old-fashioned velvet jewellery box — he looked at the brooches and rings, the pearl necklace and the earrings and a locket with a picture of Guy at three with curls and a lace collar.

He mourned his mother's death and grew quite pale and thin but gradually his work and his normal routine made him carry on quite bravely.

Gradually he went out more often to the houses of friends for birthday parties, and at Christmas, and without realizing it himself he was soon in his late forties. It was about then that he met a young Indian girl. A working girl who lived by herself. They kept meeting at mutual friends' houses and they began to enjoy each other's company. She wasn't really a girl anymore but a great many years younger than Guy. Gradually they began to go to concerts and art exhibitions together. He took her walking at weekends occasionally but she had very delicate ankles and could not manage to keep up with him and began to be afraid of the heights he climbed to. The walks stopped but they now were always seen as a couple, a fixture. People would never dream of asking the one without the other. Guy began to guide her in her reading — he made her read all his favourite authors, Jane Austen, Elizabeth Gaskell and L.P. Hartley. And her taste for fine etchings and landscapes grew as he talked to her and showed her reprints. He himself had begun to collect Indian art by little-known artists.

Guy did propose marriage to his young friend but she refused him. Later when she suggested the same to him he refused thinking the age difference was far too great and why spoil a fine friendship, a fine companionship. They made a very handsome couple. He was tall and slim with very fine blue eyes and she delicate and small always in her immaculate saris and her beautiful long hair. Gradually there came elegant strands of grey in the coiled hair.

Over the years he gave her pieces of his mother's jewellery, one year a necklace, another a brooch and the rings one by one. In that last year of his life he gave her a little velvet box and told her not to open it till her birthday. He must have had some sort of premonition. Their lives were so beautifully ordered till the day he slipped and fell while helping her down the carpeted staircase of the Club. He was never quite himself after that fall. It was January. He had broken his hip and found it difficult to walk even after it healed. She helped him to move from his bachelor home to her home to look after him. There was a physiotherapist each morning to help him with his exercises and a nurse when he became weaker in every way. In the corner of the dark hall there was a wheelchair in readiness. His favourite journals still came reminding him of the climbs and walks he still hadn't done.

He read and read each day sitting on the balcony waiting for her to come back from work. On the balcony he watched each day a stately beautiful mansion being razed to the ground. First the great booming sound with great deep echoes and then the steady hammers pounding away at the walls and the floors. Bang and then bang. Bang and then bang. Guy watched as the delicate stone work in the turrets of the terrace broke and fell on to the ground below and all the beautifully carved water spouts, then the balconies. The great terrace was down and all the bougainvilleas were covered with the grey white dust. Now only a slim tower remained to remind him of the height of that mansion.

Then they destroyed the first floor. Then the ground floor. Still the tower remained. All the doors and windows were removed and stacked up under the great wild almond trees leaving yawning dark holes. Then they started on the outhouses and the beautiful stone and marble fountain with its statue of a mermaid on a rock at the centre. One morning they attacked the single slim tower and when they had banged away at the outer shell, he saw it was an old-fashioned lift with wrought iron doors. The same artist, Guy thought, who had designed the great gates of the mansion. Who had lived here, for years and years, graciously caring for the beauty of the house and the gardens and the trees and the fountain? Who had gone up and down that lift? He hoped they were all dead and would never have to see the desecration and careless breaking of their home. Each day Guy sat on the balcony and watched this terrible, unnecessary thing being done. He hated the large crude men who came in flashy cars to see, each day, how much work was still to be done. Already planning how many wretched flats they could build cramming the place with little matchbox flats with hardly any windows and no balconies. Soon saris and grey towels would hang out from every nook and cranny. Guy knew he would not see this himself, but he had watched and knew how his beloved Bombay had changed so much since 1930.

One day he decided to make his will and he left everything to his dearest friend. He had no relatives anywhere. He read and read everything he had loved and soon the monsoons came and he could not sit on the balcony any more. In the late evenings he and she talked of going to Bath in the summer. And they thought about a river cruise down the Nile, of a trip to Yugoslavia. Peaceful evenings even as his legs grew weaker and weaker.

And then he caught a cold from his careless nurse and it quickly turned into pneumonia. There was nothing then but to take him to hospital. He struggled and he fought and everything that could be done was done but one evening very late he died. She had spent so many nights in a plastic chair outside the ICU dozing and dreaming that she could hardly understand when they told her he was dead. She sleepwalked through the choosing of the coffin and the funeral and the many friends who came to mourn this delicate serious man. She answered all the letters that came, and went to his bachelor house and packed up everything and gave away his hiking boots and great woollen socks and his sleeping bag and his rucksack.

One Sunday with the urn and his ashes she went to the nearest hill station and struggling to the highest point she scattered them in the wind. Now he will really rest, she thought.

And in her home she got rid of the wheelchair and the walker and all the "bad part" and realized that tomorrow was her birthday. She took the little velvet box out of the cupboard and opened it and inside there was an enamel locket with a picture of Guy aged three with curls and a lace collar. She put it on and it is still there. She stopped going to concerts and art exhibitions but she sat in his rocking chair and read and reread all of Jane Austen and Elizabeth Gaskell and L.P. Hartley. As she rocked she thought I never knew about his other life really. His English life or his publishing life or his long walks. Not really. We were really rather different people, but I know that he chose me and I am grateful that we had a long and fruitful friendship, a loving and delicate friendship and now I don't have anyone.

I do not have my best friend, my loyal and beloved friend, who helped me through everything that happened to me.

And outside her balcony a new, ugly, grey high-rise began to block Guy's view of the sky and the distant hills.

3   *Golden Beach Boys —*
Class of '60

The great church door closed with a crash as the last mourner came into the dark cool interior wearing filthy shorts and a black singlet — burnt and dry almost black skin and matted hair in a long plait and nothing on his feet. Bare dirty feet. Everybody knew him and watched as he came to the very front of the church and placed a handful of shells on the coffin. Instead of flowers. Most of the congregation of mourners even in the heat of May in Goa were in dark suits and dark dresses and one man wore a dazzling white suit and white shoes, white hair and a carnation in his buttonhole. The congregation had looked up momentarily, then shocked, looked down again. There would be a great deal to talk about later at the wake. In the very first pew a very old woman sat upright and the young wife and small boy wept and then were silent as the priest intoned, "Man that is born of woman hath but a short while to live."

The young boy, the dead man's son read, "Men are we, and must grieve when even the shade of that which once was great is passed away."

Soon it was over and everyone filed out of the church and the old mother leaning on the arms of distant cousins thanked each of them and asked them to her home for the wake. "We will drink a glass of wine together, please come, he would have wanted it, he will be with us, please come."

And they drank wine handed around by little women in dark dresses, distant cousins all. Some nibbled at the eats and used their napkins to wipe away stray tears and crumbs. The old mother sat upright in her own carved chair and from time to time allowed herself to speak of her great grief, "So what must I continue to live for, what? So when will I be called? All my boys gone. All lost. And this the youngest and the best. All my boys lost or murdered or dead. It's all the same. He was my golden boy, beautiful as a girl, slender and of such sweetness and goodness. 'If we sew back the wings will the butterfly fly again, flash in the sunlight?' Such questions he asked as a child. I will look after you mama, he said, when his papa died. I told him don't worry and stress yourself, but that's what he did all his life, worried for me, worried for his wife, for his child, for his friends. Worry has killed him. He worried for the old ancestral home, for the carved beautiful furniture. I told him these things mean nothing to me, they are beautiful but they are only things, I only care for you — but still he carved wood and made furniture so we could keep the house, keep the rooms and the high ceilings but for what? Nobody to live here, no laughter, no talk, we are all dead now. 'Copy this old chair for me, one customer would say, another would order a new chair to look three hundred years old. How his eyes must have ached with all those bird wings and ferns and fruit he carved for those customers. Do you remember his grey eyes searching the wood, smoothing, papering, moulding, and that great birthmark on his cheek, angry against the pale delicate skin? Nobody needs to listen to me but I need to speak. There is so much to say, so much to grieve for. Look at his wife hugging the small boy, she will have an even longer widowhood than I had."

The distant cousins fluttered around her and tried to stop the torrent of sadness but she could not stop. And why should she? "I should last so long? For what? For whom? I should go to some high mountain and be left there till death comes. I read in a book, in Japan, the old people are taken up to a tall mountain. Set the young people free, with no burdens, no regrets, no guilt." The distant cousins now really shocked contemplating this terrible barbarian rite of passage, dabbed their flushed faces, their lightly powdered cheeks with delicate, embroidered handkerchiefs.

The doctor in his white suit and white shoes and carnation who had been watching the old woman all this time, all his life really, came forward and took her hand and sat down close to her and said, "Dona Almira, let us speak of a different past. Let all this go, do not cling. Let him go, let him have a safe and quick crossing to the other land." The old woman became quiet and said he was right. "Stay with me now." And he stayed and they thought of the old days. In the old days they had always been young. Now it was different and he had no medicines for old age. He had only words of cold comfort to offer to those who might still listen. He was vain about his white healthy hair and moustache, next year he might try a beard but he looked down at his hands and saw how, though they were beautiful, they were mottled and wrinkled, with liver spots. He had delivered Dona Almira's son, the one who lay dead. He remembered the hour, he remembered the beautiful Dona Almira in labour for twelve hours and finally the delicate beautiful boy with a huge dark red stain on his cheek. That little baby was the young man dead in his coffin. "We bring so much into this world, and we leave only grieving and sadness," he sipped his wine and thought his thoughts. Helping Dona Almira with a terribly difficult birth had not been his first encounter with her. Long before that in a hot square with hundreds of pigeons a young woman in pink walked with a pink lace parasol. She looked cool and the pigeons allowed her a path. She was with her husband on their honeymoon and the young student doctor had had a coffee with them and had fallen in love for the first, last and only time in his life. He had used his doctoring in the place where she lived so that he could see her, be close and far from her all his life. Recently he had seen *Death in Venice* and been greatly disturbed by it and now had darker visions of Venice and its black gondolas. He would never go back to Venice again, never see the pigeons mulling around the beautiful Dona Almira with her pink parasol. He pressed her hand now and said, "May I bring you something Dona Almira?" And she smiled and said, "No, only stay with me and let us dream of a better time, how young we were and I may speak of a time when I fell in love with a very young doctor, in Venice, in San Marco's square. There were hundreds of pigeons and I had a new pink parasol. Mama had made me a lace parasol of palest pink lace — the door that was opened to me was also closed because it was my honeymoon. I had fallen in love. Did you know? Did you guess?" The old doctor said, "I only hoped," and he looked down at his pale pink carnation and saw the blinding sun, grey and white noisy, pushy, greedy pigeons and a pale pink parasol. And he was silent. Dreamed of a past. Now they were very old. There was no future. Only a long view of the past. So now they thought of the young man who was dead and was not their son but the son they had both hoped to have had. They shared a warmth and a great closeness known only to them and no one else in the whole wide world. They watched a group who stood together, the closest friends and now separated because the youngest of their group was dead. They too sipped their wine and thought "Yes of all of us, he did something with his life — he was a master craftsman." Each of them had built something in dreams, nothing concrete; the architect had built only a pleasure park and decorated a cafe on the streets. Another had built no bridges across great rivers. He had only sketched dozens and dozens and talked his youth and prime away. The third of the group, was to have been a great heart surgeon but no hospital had even the equipment, so his hands and dreams were nothing. He now talked, and sometimes mended a broken arm, a twisted ankle. Now as they drank to friendships and the death of their friend, they knew the truth about themselves. They had wasted their substance not on the desert air but on the golden beaches of Goa, drinking, drugging, anything but working and now they were like their friend who had come to the funeral in filthy shorts and black singlet, no shoes, long matted pigtail and needle marks up and down the veins of his arms and legs. At least he did not pretend to be something other, like them in their conventional dark suits, carefully shaved and with polished shoes and he had come to the right church, on the right day, at the right time, with shells, not flowers.

This particular death had shown most clearly what they were. They were not golden boys. They were an ageing group of old-young men who had done nothing with their lives. Only talked. Only dreamed. Only allowed the years to pass and pass them by. Years of meeting on the golden beach and talking and dreaming and singing and drinking till the sun sank into the sea. Each day the same. Except for the youngest who was now dead. He had not talked or smoked or been given to drinking. He had only listened to them and wondered and listened some more. He had believed in their talk and in their dreams and always believed that one day they would actually do something with their days and months and years. After a long while inspite of his sweetness they had grown to resent him for joining them because he was working hard each day and night, designing and carving furniture, first in a little old garage and converted shed and then hiring men to help him in his own large workshop. He made them feel guilty. He made them feel ashamed. And then came the first hippies with their drugs and their free ways and they joined them on their home ground, the golden beaches of Goa. They succumbed to this bewitching life because they could be lifted and carried away, the drugs removed their pain, their inadequacies. They could lean and dream, they could dream and lean all day long. The years as is their habit passed by. Now the real golden boy was dead and they were just beach bums. Nothing golden about them any more. Except the worn-out voice of the one who struck a chord on his guitar and sang the song of ultimate nostalgia, "Those were the days, my friends. We thought they'd never end. We'd sing and dance forever and a day. We'd fight and never lose, those were the days my friends those were the days —" The filthy pigtailed man suddenly threw his glass down and said, "Why him and not us — it's all unfair — life's a bitch and then you die." A distant cousin greatly shocked, moved forward and picked up the broken beautiful glass and said, "Whatever your distress, think of Dona Almira and how she suffers." And the group of friends wanted to shove her away — what could she know, she had hardly known their friend but they acknowledged what she said because they saw the young wife begin to weep again.

Afterwards

Many years later, a quiet scholarly young man went to his professor and said he would like to work on his thesis and the subject he had chosen was the strange phenomena that had occurred during the '60s in Goa, a former Portuguese territory in India. He and his professor talked for a long while and the older guide said at last, "Well, these things work in different ways in different countries of the world. Think of our very own lost generation, of African states taking to great primitive violence. Maybe the problem in Goa was the drug problem, the permissive cult, the inability for many years to move, to act, to do."

The young man said, "I'd like to work on it, it was our very own lost generation."

And his guide said, "You had no anger against Vietnam but you have, do you not, a strange term and reality called susagäd, maybe that had something to do with it — it's a good topic for research, just now it's a mere footnote. I should go ahead and put it on the map. By the way were you personally involved?"

The young man said, "Yes, sir, all my father's closest friends, the class of '60."

"And your father, he escaped all that?"

"Yes, my father was older and wiser even though he was the youngest he did escape all that; but he died very young — so —"

"Yes, I see," said the professor, "I think you should work on this and start with your own earliest memories —"

The young man thought, yes, first I will work on my memories and all the images of the past, of things said and done. I think papa's funeral might be a good starting point. All those strange men, papa's mourners, the man with the pigtail who came in last to the church and put shells on the coffin instead of flowers and later broke a wine glass and shouted, "Life's a bitch and then you die." And the doctor in white talking to Avo, and holding her hand. He had a flower in his buttonhole. And a friend sang *'Those were the days my friends, We thought they'd never end...'* Yes, I will start with the funeral and then the wake and I will talk to people who remember or who think they remember about those times and I will learn something and perhaps leave something behind that is worthwhile about papa's times in the scheme of things. I shall call it the *Golden Beach Boys/Class of '60:* A Phenomenon.

4

Go Down to Kew in Lilac-time

(it isn't far from London)

The day they pulled out all the tubes on the baby was the day Aneek went to Kew Gardens; it was also the day she enrolled for two weeks at a summer school in the Cotswolds. She went to Kew Gardens because the mother of the baby asked her to, and she enrolled for summer school because she needed to. That was quite a day.

The tubes had been crisscrossed over the baby's small body, mouth, nose and the tiny veins in her feet for six weeks. Just the night before the experts and the parents met and decided, "that's it — no more." And signed papers. The mother had come to her baby in the glass case for all of those six weeks and stayed with the baby gazing at her through the glass. When she went out to get a cup of coffee or water, waiting mothers gave advice. Said she shouldn't, she shouldn't be bonding with the baby — she'll be losing it in the end, they said. The mother knew better than the others, she knew she had lost it in the beginning. Last year she had lost her first baby. She felt an old hand at this recognition. When this baby had first been placed in her arms, she had known, it had somehow had the same feel to it. The nurse had looked very kind and the pale blue walls had stared down at her. Out in

Kew she had said to the nurse Aneek, "I knew this baby was going to die as well. I was going to lose her too. I'm glad I've brought her to Kew. I'd like her to have known some beautiful place, somewhere other than the intensive care unit for special babies. She is a special baby and she lived for six weeks, and that's a long time. That's forty-two days and nights and today she smiled. Will you watch her while I go to sleep? I feel very tired. I have not felt like this for six weeks." The mother slept for two whole hours without moving and the leaves of the copper beech moved above them and around them like a benediction. Aneek began to feel drowsy too, she'd been up all night because of the decision about the baby. But she watched the two of them carefully because for six weeks she had grown to be a part of the final separation. Normally she would have gone home, had a bath and gone to bed and slept for eight hours but not today. It was there on the grass, under the tree and the sun through the leaves as she watched the baby and the mother that Aneek made up her mind. After this summer she'd sort out her life. For now she'd go back to school, she'd go to summer school, she'd study and read and write and be with people of all sorts. Not with babies and their mothers. Not with babies who mostly died and their mums who were left with nothing to carry home. Trees and grass and the sun. The decision was made. The baby wasn't going to live long now. Now the tubes were out. But the baby had smiled. And no, it wasn't wind. It was a smile in Kew under the leaves of an immense copper beech. And the exhausted mother had smiled in recognition and said, "Now we really know each other and so now I can let her go." She had said this before she went to sleep. Aneek and the mother had taken turns carrying the baby in its carrycot. Aneek had carried her in the tube, and in the long queue, the mother had carried her. They had passed the roses and gone past the great Victorian Palm house making straight for the trees near the lake. They had laid out a blanket doubled and placed the baby on that. They covered her with a white shawl and it was then that it had happened. They had both been leaning over the baby and she was staring at her mother. Then she had smiled. Aneek was so glad to have been asked to come to Kew. She had been afraid but also greatly privileged. But now she began to feel a great sadness as though the sun was covered by a cloud. She got up and walked towards the lake. Willow trees bent to the water, reeds bent to the water and a serene swan floated by. Life was beastly, unfair. Aneek remembered a long ago advertisement which had said, "Life's a bitch — and then you die." This baby was going to die and her mother had brought her to Kew. What do you say about that? She'd been a nurse for a long time now but she never got over deaths. She never got over difficult births. She felt she'd be a good nurse when she stopped thinking about the pain and the suffering and the unfairness. She should just think about the nursing and not getting close to the babies or their mothers. Just cases. Cases in small glass cases, in the I.C.U. of a London hospital. She was a nurse, and it was a good job too. For an Indian woman who felt old and faded already at twenty-nine. She walked back to the small group under the great tree and the mother was still profoundly asleep. Later they had a while to wait for the train to London so they went next door to a pub called the Flower and Tirken and had a couple of G & T's and sandwiches and caught the train back. Aneek went to Islington to help the mother and the baby. She kissed the baby's perfect small hands and hugged the mother and ran down the steps back to the station. She passed Duncan Terrace where a pale blue plaque said Charles Lamb had lived there for four years. Aneek wondered if it was before Mary had stabbed their mother or after. She was terrible on dates. Good on the gory, sad details. The sun was still warm and great baskets of purple pansies and pink ploppy petunias hung from lampposts and shop fronts and Aneek thought

why should an infant die in spring,
when butterflies are on the wing,
green grass and such a sky,
why should an infant die in spring.

She thought she would go and enroll now before she lost the need. Just two weeks in the country where she would brush up on stuff, clear the cobwebs and then decide on her life. She'd worked hard and saved hard. Two weeks is what she felt her life depended on. It went well at the enrolment place though there was a large group waiting while the woman shuffled papers and files. Then it was Aneek's turn. "And what courses would you like to do?"

"Bereavement and the pre-Raphaelites and...."

"All right, that's fine — here are some brochures and forms to fill in. You forgather at Paddington station if you are going with the group or arrive on your own by Sunday evening. Bye and goodluck." Aneek felt so lucky she went off to Woolworth's and bought some spoons. She'd chucked out her last two with the trash and hadn't felt like scrabbling about for them. She bought six with the disciples on them and she bought some yellow flowers.

In her tiny flat she put the flowers in a milk bottle and washed her new good-luck spoons and laid out her summer clothes on the bed. Later, she started on the forms and looked at the coloured photographs of the school in the Cotswolds where the summer school would be happening. Then she filled up the first of the forms:—

Name	:	Aneek Setalvad
Place of Birth	:	Bombay (India)
Country of Origin	:	India
Profession	:	Nursing
Address	:	4, Kendal Street, London W1
Tel No	:	I wish

Before she went to sleep Aneek heard the mother say, "It's so lovely to hold her body without all those tubes and wires and things, she's so real to me. How can she be so perfect and have so much not working for her." She had said that in Kew and the leaves of the copper beech had moved over her face, shadows of colour on her pale intelligent face. There was still so much she would have to face. The loving and the certain death of her baby. Aneek thought "Well, in spite of everything its been a very important day for me, I'm glad I'm a nurse. I'm glad I can help even just a little, I'm glad she wanted me to go with her to Kew. I'm glad I went." Though there was still a whole week to summer school she decided to pack next day so she'd be ready and not change her mind. Having decided that the two weeks would be really warm, she packed her summer dresses and couple of cotton skirts and her sandals and cleaned her old plimsoles. I'll take my mack just in case, but I dare it to rain. As she packed she felt very excited and on the edge of something new, a new journey, a turning point. She packed her Yeats and the Shakespeare's Sonnets and her Bible. Whatever happens I'll have my three favourite books with me. And now she was really ready. Ready for anything. Her father would have said, "Ready for any eventuality." Like Kew Gardens there has to be a life outside the Intensive Care Unit of a hospital.

On the day she arrived at Stroud, she had walked to the school from the station. She walked up with a young man who had got into the train when it stopped at Swindon. Till he got in, Aneek had been thinking about how such quiet country lanes with their neat hedgerows and little cottages could produce so much violence against little children. How could such peacefulness hide such cruelty. There had been a spate of dreadful murders that week and they had all happened in surroundings like the ones the train passed even now. She did not read the book on her lap. When the young man got in she watched him. He had very blue eyes and lovely hands and he was reading a book she had admired greatly. Aneek wondered what he thought of it and wanted to know. By now everyone in India would be asking questions and sharing food. The English were so quiet and reserved. Perhaps now she preferred this to the general curiosity and noise and friendliness of the Indian scene in a train compartment. Now, as they walked to the school, they talked and she told him something about the difference in behaviour in railway compartments. She said she must be a lot like them at home because she had been curious about his reaction to the book he was reading. He said he didn't like it so much as being very disturbed about it and admired the writing which was so contained and slightly aloof, inspite or because the events were so terrible. He found the *Ghost Road* unbearably moving. He asked what she had planned to read. Aneek blushed at the thought of the unread book on her lap, an old favourite. "I read it almost every year, it's called *The Transit of Venus."* And he said, "I know it and like it very much. Do you know her other work — she's unusually un-Australian, isn't she?" Aneek asked him if he'd ever been to the Costwolds before and he said, "Oh, I practically grew up here, I was in the care of an aunt. Part of the reason I chose to come here this summer." She asked him what courses he was taking up for the two weeks and he said, well, actually he was one of the lecturers. That had pulled her up short. He seemed so young. She had always thought of teachers as being so much older. And then she remembered that after all these were mid-career courses and maybe she was older than he was. After a while some others caught up and she went on ahead.

The gates, when they reached, were beautiful wrought iron and there were lawns. A vast playing field and then the scrunchy driveway arrived at the yellowish stone building of the school itself. It was a middling large girls' boarding school loaned for the summer school. This was all theirs for two whole weeks. As they climbed the gracious steps with two vast stone urns on pillars groaning with flowers, the sun still shone. A good omen. After coffee, there were more forms to be filled in, meeting the teachers, generally inspecting the rooms and the class-rooms. Aneek met the young man from the train. He was to take the course on "Bereavement."

"Why are you taking this course?" he asked her and she said, "To learn how to deal with the deaths of infants and to try and help their mothers really. To help them cope and not be overwhelmed myself. To understand the whole process of grieving." From her timetable she saw she would be meeting Kim Walken's class five mornings a week from eleven to twelve. So I shall see him ten times at least before I leave she thought. She wondered what she would say about why she chose the pre-Raphaelites for one of her other courses. She would say because I love their sad romantic love of love and old myths and legends. I love the way they viewed their models and their great beauty. She loved their poetry and their painting and their view of crafts and reviving them. One day she planned to afford William Morris wallpaper. She went often when the weather was good to the Tate walking by the river and then looking at the Rosetti's and Millais and Burne-Jones. All that longing and waiting and lush auburn curling hair. Aneek realized she was humming as she found her room and chose the bed by the window and put her three books on her desk with paper and pencils. She unpacked. The learning started the next day. She waited. She looked out of the wide window at the lawn and trees. She thought about the mother and the baby in Kew Gardens and knew that all this had started that day. She found the telephone and rang up the mother in Islington though she knew even before she was told. "Take care," she said, "take care of yourself, allow yourself to grieve, allow yourself to cry and howl and be angry." The voice on the phone was very controlled, very English and thanked her for thinking of her. Aneek thought of the mother's pale face sleeping and the shadows of the beech leaves passing over her face.

The class was very quiet. There was the sound of a fly or bee or something with wings against the windowpanes. Aneek looked out of the window at another copper beech and thought of the mother in Kew. She was thinking of her in the context of the opening remarks of Kim Walken when he had said, "When a love tie is severed, a reaction, emotional and behavioural, is set in train, which we call grief. My lectures are about grief; more particularly about what happens to the survivors when a person dies." He walked to the window and helped the butterfly to fly away. It had been trapped all this while. The class shifted in their chairs. He returned to his desk and said, "The loss of a parent, the loss of a husband or wife or child, is one of the most severe forms of psychological stress, yet it is one that many of us can expect to undergo at some time in our lives. At other times we may be expected to give comfort and support to relatives or friends who are themselves bereaved. Grief, like any other aspect of human behaviour, is capable of description and study, and when studied it turns out to be as fascinating as any other psychological phenomena." He paused and looked at the faces in front of him. Kim Walken looking at the faces in front of him, saw really only one face and remembered:

> How can I, that girl standing there,
> My attention fix
> On Roman or on Russian
> Or on Spanish politics?

Aneek was thinking, yes, it's their eyes, it's their eyes that I can never get used to, even after all these years. All those different greys and greens and blues, some like pale glass. As a child she had collected marbles. Kim

Walken's are very blue. In India eyes are nearly always brown or black. It's a real shock when they are green or grey: she came back to what Kim Walken was saying and she bent her head and jotted something down on the pad in front of her. The hour slipped by so quickly. It felt full of a great deal of things to think about. And she thought about Kew Gardens and the mother and the baby who had smiled and about bereavement. She wanted the hour to prolong itself. She didn't want to leave the room. She didn't want him to leave.

Aneek worked hard all week only allowing herself a long walk in the evenings. Sometimes the lecturers walked too and quite often she found herself walking with Kim. On the Friday evening he asked her if she would like to walk with him to a village called Bisley. His aunt lived there. "It's a long walk but a really good walk," he said, "and you will get a really fine idea of this county and all it has to offer." Of course she said yes and the next day they set off quite early. Aneek felt quite easy with him having listened to him five hours that week. "Won't your aunt mind your bringing a stranger — she must look forward to your visits."

"Why on earth should she mind? She's a lonely person and very dear to me. She has to like you as I do. She lives by herself with a dog called Perdita and she's the most self-sufficient person I know. We are very close. When my parents died I was just a boy, she brought me up and was mother and father to me. Really, she left me to get on with things mainly supplying me with warmth and affection so I never felt an orphan." Again, the day was wonderfully warm and they walked on little paths and bigger lanes and crossed several fields, stopping once near a stream to cool their faces. Kim knew his way as though he walked this way everyday. "Oh, I rambled about, all my childhood. I can't ever forget it. Aunt Meg did a lot of walking with me. She's wracked by a bad knee now and is confined to her garden really." At one of the charming crossroads some children were selling wild flowers and Aneek bought a huge bunch for Aunt Meg. Kim said she'd love them. His Aunt Meg was a rather fine watercolourist and she painted flowers. "In fact, that's how she manages her finances. People come to her to buy her paintings. She never has to stir out of the house. Thank God her cottage belongs to her." They were now quite close to the cottage. They still had a small wood and a gentle hillside left. "My aunt has a cow and of course Perdita and me. I hope Perdita lives forever and she has me always." He re-marked what a good walker Aneek was and had she done any climbing? To which she said no as she was frightened of heights. He told her he was taking a group of boys for a bit of climbing in Wales after the summer school was over. Aneek began to miss him already. She realized he had a whole life of his own. She was just an accident in it. And then Kim said, "Look I know it's a bit sudden but I feel sudden and want to know if when I come back from Wales I could see you again. I'd love to take you on the river to my favourite village, quite near London. This weather is sure to last. It's a pity to waste it." Aneek in a daze said, "Yes" and again "Yes, I'd love it." They had walked through the tree dark wood and then sunlight again at the hill overlooking the cottage. The hill had five painted black and white cows lying on it and a great brown bull and then the sloping orchard and garden. The cottage itself was of the same honey yellow that was used for all the buildings and had wisteria and honeysuckle growing over it. The old boundary wall had a creeping pale pink wild rose climbing thickly. The air smelt of summer and flowers and there was the sound only of bees and an occasional bird. They almost ran down the last bit and found Aunt Meg stirring marmalade and staring out of her kitchen window. She hugged Kim and said "I was thinking of you and here you are! I'm so glad you've come nice and early so we'll have a long day together." She thanked Aneek for her flowers and found a large jam jar for them. "I used to pick flowers like these on my rambles. Alas, no more!" she said wistfully. She was a striking tall woman with grey white hair and the same intense blue eyes that Kim had. They sat on a stone bench warmed by the sun drinking coffee and taking in her garden. It was wild and yet ordered. There was a large stone dog to guard them as "Perdita seems to be chasing sheep this morning." There was also a stone porcupine and tortoise, a sun dial and the stone birdbaths, one with a dolphin base and the other a mermaid. At the far end of the garden near the main gate was a splendid copper beech. Aneek thought, when I think of this summer I will always think of copper beeches and whenever I see a copper beech I will think of these days, this summer and the one in Kew, the one in the garden, at the school and now at aunt Meg's. She was intensely happy but also sad because it would all end so soon. She said to Aunt Meg, "You have a garden of such surprises — it's so beautiful, your garden." Aunt Meg said, "It's my pride and joy and with Kim and Perdita added, truly my cup runneth over — Kim, why not stay the night, leave tomorrow. Do you have classes later today? I haven't seen a soul for ages.

Do stay. Ring them up. I always have spare toothbrushes. I'll go in and give that marmalade a good stir while you decide, then we'll think about lunch." Kim turned to Aneek and said, "Whatever you decide we'll do," and she said, Yes, she'd like to stay very much. For a while she didn't think any more about things ending. She was here and Kim was here and they had lots of time. There was tomorrow and then another whole week. It was such bounty and had come out of nowhere. They had a lazy, do-nothing sort of day and in the evening a "comfort" fire, Aunt Meg called it because it had turned slightly chilly; it wasn't really cold at all. Aunt Meg, "Call me Meg," she had said, asked her many questions which she found she enjoyed answering. She realized how little she really talked to people. She told them about summers back home in Delhi where she grew up. The fierce heat and the great hot winds of dust that built up and how fans were so inadequate they just pushed the hot air around. She told them of the doors made of a fragrant cooling root, which were splashed with water and kept the rooms cool and smelling wonderful.

She told them how the gardener each evening watered the lawns so that the earth smelled cool and how they all slept under mosquito nets in a neat row on the lawn. She told them of the splendour of summer flowering trees, of the gulmohur and the jacaranda and laburnam and the acacia. She told them about eating mangoes and her mother's crisp cotton saris and how everything waited for the rains to come and when they finally did come, there were tremendous storms and mighty gales, and dams burst and rivers overflowed their banks and there were floods and so much death by water, collapsed houses and walls. How day after day sheets of rain would pour down till everything seemed annihilated, wonderful trees were uprooted and everything was the colour grey-brown. Nothing dried, fungus ruining books and all articles of leather. Awful smells of decaying matter with children jumping into filthy water ponds and puddles everywhere. And then came the waterborne diseases. She told them how every season was so overdramatic and how they never had spring or autumn. "Here it is mild, except your winters of course." She got up and looked out of the windows — it was still a long twilight, shadows creeping over the lawn. She shivered but not because it was cold. They asked her about her hospital work and she told them about the babies in their glass cases and their waiting expectant mothers. They listened as it grew dark outside and then she told them about Kew Gardens and the baby who had smiled at her mother. They were all quiet for a bit and then Meg said, "You must come to me whenever you want, alone if Kim can't come. Will you do that? You don't even have to ring me. I'm always here." They watched a programme on television about John Betjeman's boyhood and his hated boarding school. It was so bleak and accurate, the images about that particular loneliness and the pain of it welled up in her till she could smell the polish and disinfectant of her years in boarding school. It had been up in the hills of Simla, a school run by Irish nuns. All the time she had been very cold and lonely and homesick. She remembered in the playground standing in a tiny patch of sunlight staring down at the dark valley below. She had been very frightened of two nuns in particular and the matron of the junior school. She had been forced to eat meat. She has never eaten meat since.

The TV programme showed the cold refectory with no sunlight filtering through the musty locker rooms and the cold long dark dormitory with its shadows. She felt even now what Betjeman must have felt. She wondered if Kim's lectures about grief were all just theory. How do people ever really get over the death of a beloved one? Why, she couldn't even slough off the dread and fear, the sad weight of a hated boarding school. "School can be so awful when you are little it can last all your life if it has really been bad. And I suppose it can also be a good and very happy time," she thought of Angela Brazil. They ate chocolate biscuits and drank their comforting tea. She told them that even after all these years she could remember only the names and faces of the two nuns she feared most and the matron of the junior school — Mother Cecilia and Mother Baptista and Miss Thomas. Not a single name of a friend. She told them how once her father had visited and brought her a box of chocolates and how hard she had tried not to show how she felt but how finally he had watched helplessly as she cried into that open box. The head nun, steely grey eyes and dragging right leg, had tapped her cane and said, "She's doing very well, there's nothing to worry about," and her scream withheld, as her father left down the long driveway. Such terrible fears when one is a child. And Kim asked, "Do the nightmares persist?" and Aneek said, "Yes! They continue even now with all these years in between and no nuns." And she was surprised that he had guessed.

Aneek's room was up in the attic, small and warm with a sloping roof and the smell of the climbing rose just outside the window. She could see the hillside with its five painted cows and the brown bull and the dark wooded area above. In the bookcase she found old editions of 'Milly Molly Mandy' and the 'William' books and Laurie Lee and Flora Thompson. All Aneek's favourite books over the years. "How odd my life has been, and is. There must be so many people like me who are odd and all because the English colonized us and gave us their language. We are accidents of history and so many of us are comfortable with that accident. I love these books, I love this countryside, I love Meg and Kim and the mother and baby in Kew. I'm Indian but I love this place more than India. India was only Ma and Papa and now they are gone there's nothing there to draw me back. So what does it make me? I won't think of that now, only this peaceful home and the bright squares of this cotton quilt."

Next morning, looking out of the window with its small panes she saw birds wheeling in a blue sky, the five painted cows still there and the sun was up. She and Kim went to fetch the milk and took a longish way home. He pointed out the valley in the middle distance where Laurie Lee's cottage was and he picked a buttercup and held it under Aneek's chin and asked, "But could you live here and not go back to India?" And she said, "Yes, all things considered I could, I love it here and with you here I have a friend."

"I am here", he said, "and now let's get back. I want to mow the lawn and fetch some wood before we go back. Come on, lots to do." She sat in the sun-warmed pile of grass and then they took it down to the cow in her shed, piled logs of wood near the grate after cleaning it and generally made themselves do chores difficult for Meg.

Soon after lunch they left and Meg made them promise to come next weekend if they could and before their "real" lives began again. "We'll have a picnic in the orchard if the weather holds. Promise to come," and they promised to, if all was well.

The next week was work and lectures and walks every evening and then Saturday came and they went back to Bisley. This time they took Meg to a pub for pub grub saving the picnic for Sunday. It couldn't have been warmer or more blessed. They had a wonderful time drinking a great many G and T's and Aneek got quite high and Kim said, "You are quite a soak, Aneek," and she said, "Yes I'm happy, so happy to be with Meg and you, and now you are both honourable members of my family."

The next day they had their picnic in the orchard among the old apple and pear trees and the one old medlar tree. This time Perdita stayed with them all afternoon. Meg went in when the sun was low over the horizon. "Race you to the far wall and back," Aneek said and they ran and ran and reached the wall together and Kim collapsed holding her and Aneek looked into his blue, blue eyes and said, "I love you dearly — like a sister and do you?"

"No," Kim said, "I love you dearly, not like a brother." He kept holding her very close.

That Sunday was over so quickly and when they got back to Stroud it was just to pack and leave in the morning. They said goodbye at the station, Aneek waiting for her train to London and Kim waiting for his group of climbers.

"I'll ring you as soon as I get back from Wales on Friday."

"Yes," Aneek said, "I'll be waiting."

"And we'll go to Cookeham Dean and Marlow. Don't forget me. Take care." And she said, "You take care, don't disappear, don't die." And the train came. Summer school was over. Back in her room she put her copper beech leaves in a bowl. They were still warm and smelt of summer. She opened all her windows thinking that there was only a week to wait, only a week. She rang Meg to thank her for all her kindness and Meg said, "You are so happy that's why you rang — I'm so glad. Kim is very lucky to have found you — and you?"

"Oh Meg, my cup runneth over, truly."

"Yes," said Meg.

One morning with ordinary things happening in the street where she lived, Aneek got off at Edgeware Road and bought some milk and some bread and came into her flat. There was a letter for her. She read it and put the milk into the fridge and went back down the stairs and into the street. They must have found her address in Kim's wallet or his diary. It was from a hospital. It was about Kim. He'd been hurt in a climbing accident in Wales. They couldn't find any near relatives so they had contacted her. She ought to come as Kim was in a coma with tubes everywhere, the monitor ticking away. It was unreal. It was familiar, saying goodbye at Stroud station she had said, "Don't disappear, don't die," and Kim had said, "You too, don't disappear, don't die." And here he was white and shaven, blue eyes closed and the sheets white and right up to his neck. Aneek took his arm and kissed his hand and each of his fingers, realizing it was the beginning of a long goodbye. And she wept for Kim and herself and wept because now nothing would ever be the same again.

As the morning dragged on she thought of another hospital and thought Kim won't die, not in a hospital like this one. This one is so clean and everything is in order and gleaming and the nursing staff so excellent, their heels clicking up and down the corridor outside. And Kim is so young. He's got everything working for him. Not like that other place. That hell called an I.C.U where they had taken her father when he'd had a stroke. That was a town in summer over two hundred miles from his home. And he'd been in a coma for over a month. Now if ever there had been a good man it was her father. She was only grateful that he would never know where he had been for a whole month. So what happens to the bad people of the earth, where are they put? The town had been dusty with filth everywhere even up close to the hospital. There had been a truck strike, there had been a municipal strike. The garbage was not removed for weeks. Negotiations were in progress. The curtains and windowpanes of the I.C.U. were filthy. The air conditioner did not work, the hospital bed was rusty and would not crank up or down — it just stayed flat. Her father's bed was curtained off from the other beds and people trooped in with food and bedpans and there didn't seem to be any doctors or nurses, there was also a doctors' strike about wearing white. Relatives ate and slept on the floors of the I.C.U. There were flies everywhere, where her father had lain, his breathing making a terrible sound. The fan blew the hot air first one side and then another. Aneek had been quite helpless to make any changes except bringing clean sheets and pillow cases and towels from home and she squeezed his orange juice herself in a juicer. This was after she caught a glimpse of the hospital kitchens and pantry. The corridors she walked all night were dirty and there were rats. All the benches had bundles of wrapped-up sleeping forms. Women with dirty mops moved them sloppily first in one direction and then another. The water in the bucket never changed. At night she heard the fearful sound of a peacock calling out.

Of course her father had died. How could anyone have survived such a place And he was not a young man. On the day he died, it had rained the first rains and all the dust became mud and slush, a river of filth, everything the colour of dirt except for the white sheets they had covered him with. That was also the day she had made up her mind to leave that country and also somewhere at the back of her mind she had decided to train to be a nurse. She felt such guilt and overwhelming sadness she felt she could have done something for her father if she had been a trained nurse. Now as she looked at the gleaming walls of this place, the clean bed, the clear panes of glass, the spotless nurses, white-coated doctors and Kim so young lying with his eyes shut, she felt hope. She took his hand again in hers and said, "Don't you die on me, don't you dare die and leave me alone. I was alone before I met you and that I could bear because I had not met you. But now if you leave me it will be a betrayal. So you fight. I'll come every day and stay as long as I am allowed to but you have to fight very hard all the time even when I am not here. I'll not bear my life without you and I know you can hear every word I say. Think of Meg, think of you, think of me and think of all we mean to do with our lives. You come out of this coma and then I'll really fight with you. I can't really help you now in the place you have gone to but come out, come back quickly. I'm here, so don't go away — don't even think it." Aneek talked to him ceaselessly believing he could hear every word she said.

After night duty in her hospital she came straight to Kim and stayed with him even when she could no longer keep her eyes open. Coaxing him, bullying him, making love to him. "I hate you Kim Walken, how could you make me love you and then go away like this? You have no right at all. So fight, you bastard. Think of never making love again; think of making love, think of walking and talking and being together. Don't give up, don't leave. I can't talk to Meg. What would I say? What would you say? What words would you find to tell her what happened. There's so much unfinished stuff. I can't do this alone. My wanting it is not enough. You have to want it badly enough." She went on like this day after day, arguing, bullying and berating him. Loving him, enraged with him, loving him to return to her. "Just press my hand ever so slightly just to say hello. Just to say goodbye. You can't possibly leave without saying goodbye, I said, 'don't disappear, don't die,' and you said, 'you too' — don't you remember?"

On the ninth day when she went to the hospital they told her that Kim had died in the night. She heard them and she kissed his hands and his mouth and she thought. "He must feel that is something we've never done enough. It's best this way but what happens to me now? Kim said, 'When a love-tie is severed what happens to the survivors?' I am a survivor. What happens to me? What do I do now?" She rang Meg who said, "Don't cry, don't cry, Aneek. Come here as soon as you can, I'll be waiting, I'm here." She packed a few things and took the train to

Stroud and tried not to think of the train journey just a few weeks ago. Outside, the fields were the same, the woods were the same. The sun still shone so warm. How had this thing happened? At Swinden the train stopped. Kim didn't get into the train. Kim didn't sit reading *The Ghost Road*. At Stroud she couldn't bear to walk all the way alone without Kim. When she reached Shermershill Meg was at the kitchen window and she waved. She came out and hugged Aneek and they wept sitting on the stone bench with Perdita and the stone dog watching them. They thought of that warm Saturday morning and the marmalade that needed stirring. Aneek was shivering with cold and shock and Meg put her to bed with brandy and two hot-water bottles and said, "You sleep now. There'll be time enough when you wake to talk and remember and to grieve." Aneek slept for many hours and woke in the dark and thought of Kim downstairs. He wasn't anywhere she could reach him. Kim was dead. She thought of the things he had planned for the weekend he came back from Wales — "I want to take you to Cookham Dean, one of my favourite villages. We'll go to the churchyard and to a pub for grub and then to Marlow. I'll row you on the river and you'll see the river and its many locks and weirs and you'll see a very old Abbey set in beautiful grounds and an old Norman church and great copper beeches and tall reeds by the water, and the swans and geese and ducks." And Aneek thought of the reeds by the lake at Kew and the baby who was alive and was dead now and she thought of her young sleeping mother. And she thought of the painting she'd seen in the Tate by Millais of Ophelia floating down the river, her gown spread wide, dotted with wild flowers and the tall reeds by the river. Aneek sat up and cried and cried and thought how selfish I am, what must poor Meg be feeling all by herself? She crept down the steps and found Meg huddled near the fire where they had sat one late evening eating chocolate biscuits and drinking their tea. She made some tea now and brought it to Meg saying, "I'm not crying for me, Meg. I'm crying for all the waste, for Kim being so young and his life. I wish he were alive. I'm crying for our lives and your life Meg, for what could have been and for that small baby who died and it's all such a waste, so much love and so much pain to pay for it. What's it all for? The young mother sleeping at last under the copper beech in Kew, sleeping because her baby had smiled at her and she knew the baby was going to die. Oh Meg, what's it all for? What's the grand plan?" And Meg brought out the old family albums and there was Kim as a child and Kim as a boy. Kim in the orchard and up a ladder, and Kim with his dog Shan and Kim and Kim and Kim. What's the point of being born and growing and loving and dying? "That's the point," Meg said, "that's precisely the point that we love and we lose what we love. You might not have met Kim. Would that have been better? Wasn't the world a happier place for containing Kim? You will now always have each other. Forever and ever. Hard as that seems just now. Impossible as that seems now to accept. Just now it's all sad, all grieving and you must mourn him or you will die or break. Tell me, Aneek, what did Kim say in his lectures on bereavement? Try and tell me, perhaps it will help us both. Try and remember, try and tell me what he said." And Aneek began to tell her, "When a love-tie is severed, a reaction, emotional and behavioural is set in train, which we call grief, more particularly my lectures are about what happens to the survivors when a person dies." They talked and wept till the light tinged the sky and when they drew apart the curtains, they could see the five black and white cows painted on the hill. The sun rose.

Gradually the year slipped along. In late August, the rains came and it became chilly and then gradually it became cold and then colder and Aneek knew that the golden summer was over outside as well as inside her. She moved between her room and sleep and the I.C.U. where she worked not thinking too much. I am a survivor of a loss because of death and I need help and there is no help, not in the way Kim spoke of helping the bereaved — I'm one of his statistics. He gave us tables of statistics. "Thirty-one in London" ages between twenty-five and sixty-five — When will my help come? Not from the hills, she thought — the hills had killed Kim. She rang Meg or Meg rang her every weekend. Meg asked her to come as soon as she was ready, the cottage was always there. "Come, you needn't even talk, come if you need the quiet and to be away from London. Come for Christmas, come for Easter or come when summer comes. But come, I need you too. Remember that."

When summer really came, it was July again and one warm Saturday morning Aneek took the train to Stroud and walked to Meg's cottage and as she came down the hill through the orchard and garden, there was Meg at the kitchen window. She waved.

The year had come full circle.

And here, she thought, I shall have my baby and I shall call my baby Altamash and I will take Altamash to Kew gardens in lilac time.

5 The Girl in a Burkha, Riding a Cycle

It was the year of teaching Jane Eyre, Henry Esmond and Yeats, also the speeches of Martin Luther King. A good year till everything changed. It was the year I had two remarkable students in my third year literature classes. I cannot tell you how rare that is and how wonderful. I mean you can have one gifted student, and you can have not one. I had always thought of them as a couple, mismatched though they were. In their first year she came on a cycle wearing a burkha always accompanied by a man with grey hair, also on a cycle. He carried her books for her. In that first year Ameena always kept her burkha on all day, a black one and sometimes pale blue, even pink. Even in the great heat with slow revolving fans she always had her head covered. In that first year of teaching collected poems and bits and pieces, the class had two fine novels in their syllabus, *Cry the Beloved Country* and *The Lord of the Flies*. The text went well, the discussions and arguments later were full of liveliness and real outrage and feeling. They were the right age to be so agonized and angry. The best discussions were always led by these two students. Ameena and Christopher. Christopher was very tall, older then the rest of the students, and a young man from the seminary. He was a very handsome young man. I suspect many of the girls were in love with him — a kind of Montgomery Clift in a cassock, in *I Confess*. There had been a rerun of *I Confess*. He had a very good mind very rational, dry, he always spoke very quietly. Ameena was a pale girl not pretty, yet. They argued a lot and brought many of those classes into lively discussions about good and evil and the cruelty of man to his fellow-men. I still remember their term papers. Somewhere I probably still have them. In their second year Ameena still came on a cycle wearing a burkha but the minute she was into the college porch she would throw it off, bundle it into her bag and run up to lectures on the second floor wearing a tidy pair of jeans and a T-shirt. Christopher was even taller now and wore a dog collar. They always sat together. They still argued and debated and felt most strongly about what they read. And so we came to the year in question. Their last year with me. Their last year of reading literature. Their last of freedom.

They saw both Jane Eyre and Henry Esmond as love stories of the most mature kind. They both loved Yeats as the most profound of twentieth century poets. They loved his political poetry and his love poetry and often saw it as the same impulse. And then one day we woke to violence. This city we all thought we knew so well. It erupted. College closed down. The meat man and the baker, both Muslims, stopped coming. Terrible stories in the newspapers, terrible images on television. We all seemed to hide not knowing what we could do. One late night a phone call came from Ameena asking me to come to the Haj house in Crawford Market, to bring blankets and food and medicines. I went, of course, the next day and found the mosque. Crowds of women and children frightened, huddled together. Afraid. Hungry. Hurt. Anguished. Their city, their homes. The place stank of sweat and of fear. I found Ameena carrying a baby whose mother could not be found. I saw Christopher bandaging an old man with a wound on his leg. It was chaos but there was so much to do. I shall never forget that morning and that afternoon and night and the days and nights that followed. Many others came to help during those anxious dreadful days. Even the man with grey hair who used to accompany Ameena to college on a cycle carrying her books. Once during a tea break I asked her who he was and she said, "My father. Didn't you know?" There was much I did not know about Ameena.

After what seemed a long while our island became quiet again, though fear remained, and suspicion remained. Our meat man came back and the bread man, long-lost friends. When college started again Ameena did not come back. Nor did Christopher. Lectures became dull. I missed them very much. I did not dare to ask. What would I have said? People whispered and often I saw Ameena's father with his cycle at the college. Sometimes good comes of evil. Peace out of violence. Sometimes we have to believe that, also sometimes we see it happening and it is rare and it is good. We have to help it. Preserve it.

Term ended. Examinations came and went. It was holidays again. I had much time to think of and I thought of Ameena and Christopher. I tried to think this when I went to see Ameena's father. It was a sad and difficult meeting.

He looked older, greyer. During the entire meeting two pigeons kept on moaning near the arch of the doorway. But I learnt much from it. He was full of grief and kept repeating, "If all this, if all this", spreading his arms out wide, "had not happened, my Ameena would not have gone away, she would not have left. She was so young, she was so old, she wanted to put everything right, one day a bleeding dog, another day the troubles in South Africa and then these terrible riots. My wives, they continue to cook and look after the children. They also feel bad but they carry on. They do not rush away leaving their homes trying to put the world to rights all by themselves. Human kind is bad and it does bad things but it is a cycle and the wheel turns and things once again become good and livable. You are her teacher, you know her. Do you have news, do you perhaps have a message from her for me?" When I had told him I knew nothing and had hoped he might know something he heaved a long sigh and said life is indeed an irony. "I wanted Ameena to marry when she was fifteen but she wanted to finish school. She made me promise only two difficult things. She wanted to go to a good college for the whole three-year course and she wanted freedom, the kind my wives did not have. I said yes to both thinking there could be no real problem with these two promises. I did keep my promise, I let her go to college for the whole three years or almost and now I have also kept my second promise. I have given her freedom. I have not tried to find her. I have not tried to bring her back. I did not know it would come about in this way, in this cruel fashion with no warning. I blame this hypocritical city, this city that pretends, this city that has been a father and mother to us since partition. We clung to her believing we were safe, that we would always be safe because it was our home. The very last time I saw Ameena she said, 'I cannot live

here any more, I cannot love this city that has undone so
many lives, that has broken every promise to its trusting
people.' But I did not realize she meant to leave the very
day her work was over at Haj house when all the people
finally went to their homes or left this city because they
no longer had homes to go to. Some of us will go on living
here but uneasily. With no trust ever again. Now that this
has happened and on such a scale we will always live in
fear, because it can happen again and again and we will
never know beforehand. You will visit her?"

And I said, "Yes, if Ameena writes to me I will go to
her. Is there some message I might take to her from you?"

And he said, "Only tell her I have her cycle safe with
me, and that I kept my promise." More than a year later
I got a postcard from Ameena, her address and a little map
showing how to get to her. She had been so near, she had
been so far.

I took the train to Karjat and started to trek upwards
for nearly half a day following Ameena's map carefully.
I reached the little crossroad which was marked with red
pencil and then listened for the sound of water — her
postcard had said, "Follow the path which sounds of
water — as in waterfall!" I soon did come to a miniature
waterfall and quite close by two mud and thatch huts,
with a kind of fence all round. One seemed a school or
a clinic. The other must contain Ameena and Christopher.
It did — and what a welcome for this tired trekker! They
looked different and yet the same. They told me I looked
different and yet the same. We ate *dal* and *roti* and a
kind of prickly vegetable and all my bars of chocolate
and energy biscuits. And I thought much good can come
of bad and in the oddest of ways. If it had not been for

all the violence and madness of that terrible January, none of this would have happened. All that terror and bloodshed, if it had not been for that, these two would not be here. We each must do what we can and as soon as we mean to do it. Their school had fifteen and a half students. They told me the children and women had work in the mornings, so school was in the afternoons. Their clinic was open all hours. "Yesterday we were midwives, three births, we learnt all manner of things during our advanced first-aid courses and the rest is common sense. The villagers are so poor. But they trust us and come to us. They have taught us much more than we have taught them."

"And you?" they asked, "What of you? We have missed you so. We wanted to wait before asking you to come. It mattered what you might think."

I told them that I was still teaching and missed them and had no other students like them. No more arguments and clashes about right and wrong and evil and good. No more, near tears. Do you remember, *Lord of the Flies*. 'His voice rose under the black smoke before the burning wreckage of the island; and infected by that emotion, the other little boys began to shake and sob too. And in the middle of them, with filthy body, matted hair, and unwiped nose, Ralph wept for the end of innocence, the darkness of man's heart, and the fall through the air of the true, wise friend called Piggy.' Do you remember? What a silence there was in the lecture room, how it was unbearable to think of it all ending as it did." We were quiet for a while.

It was late but we couldn't bear to turn in. The lamp was smoking and Ameena took it inside to deal with it and I said to Christopher, "Well, and is the world well lost and found for you?" And Christopher said, "Yes, the world is well lost and another called Ameena truly found."

They did not have much in their hut but they did have all their books.

Sensing my sadness, Ameena said, "But for you we would not be here, you must know that." Then I felt that I should feel some guilt, some blame. Christopher said, "No, no guilt and no blame but you were there at the right time for us. You shared all the thoughts in all the books with us, and you forced us to think about right and wrong and evil and pain, and you came to that terrible Haj house day after day. But for you and that black January we would not be here." I felt strangely pleased but guilty at the same time and I told of my meeting Faiz and the pigeons, and what Faiz had said, and his message. And Ameena said, "So he is sad and bitter still — he has lost so much faith and many friends and the ground under his feet. But I know he will be all right in time, I was no good for him. I'm glad he still has my cycle. Do you know he taught me to cycle? He was a kind and good man. I have so much to be grateful for. And now bed. Good night."

Next morning, a Sunday, Christopher and I went for a long walk and I said, "So Christopher, no regrets of any kind? Only asking."

"Of course, being human, even Ameena has some. Guilt mostly at hurting people who don't understand. My mother, for instance. Immediate pain and distant fears. But nothing could change this decision, this is for always. I have written to my mother; in our family all my brothers are priests. My doubts started in the seminary. The ivory tower aspect, the isolation from real needs, other people, in the context of this country how can we just be so sterile? Knowledge with no real application. For instance our order hardly helped the poor. Elitist, just good schools and excellent colleges and producing a greater and greater divide. I have written to my superiors. Silence from them. Silence from my mother. Perhaps in time she'll come round. Perhaps not. I won't change, that's all I know at the moment. And Ameena, forever Ameena, and her clear emotional responses to things. Do I answer your question, Ma'am? Isn't it beautiful? A miracle. And in the monsoons a heavy, green, dripping silence day and night and our waterfall like a rush and bursts of white continuous lightning. Ameena is a great comforter to everyone, so many painful crude accidents, all the implements of work are so heavy, so badly made, their axes and saws, their ordinary knives. Do you remember that time in the second year when Ameena brought that bleeding, dying puppy to college and tried to save its life and all that blood everywhere?"

"How could I forget? Crowds of students trying to get into the staff bathroom to see what was happening and it was Ameena crying and crying and finally wrapping the puppy up in her dupatta and begging the college *mali* to bury it in the garden. Ameena weeping bitterly and cursing those 'beastly cruel men, brutes kicking the small puppy, how I hate men, how I hate men!' It was ghastly."

"It's then that I really fell in love with Ameena. That was the day, the day of the dying pup in the upstairs staff bathroom because there wasn't any water anywhere else."

"So now you two will not ever come back, will you? Do you think that?"

"No, now we are here, who can say about ever? We took so much for granted, everything really. We were asleep, all that great poetry, just the day before the riots broke we did that Yeats, remember, 'Now days are dragon-ridden, the nightmare rides upon sleep,' now we take nothing for granted. Will you come sometimes? It gets lonely. Come for old times' sake whenever we cross your mind." And I did. Often.

6 *Item : One Calendar on Wall*

I came to this big city because I got a job in a college. It was a good time. But mostly it was a very bad time. It was good because I had a family to support and so many people do not have work that pays them anything at all. It was a good time because I, at least, was earning something. It was a good time because I had got a job in what was considered a good college.

It was a bad time because I didn't know anybody and I lived in a room in the suburbs and I spent hours travelling in trains — to work and back to that room. You will have noticed that I do not say "to work and back home". It wasn't a home. It was a room. It contained a bed, a table, a chair, a mirror and my wife. The bathroom was down two flights of stairs. The stairs and the bathroom were two things I did not allow myself to think about. But because I have mentioned them I might at least tell you why I preferred never to think about them. The stairs were, at all times, foul-smelling and always unlit. Perhaps this was a good thing because, at all times, the stairs could contain anything from human pee, excreta, snot, ordinary spittle, or *paan* spittle. The bathroom was shared by all the tenants of the building. The floor of this room was always wet — not water wet but almost ankle-deep in all the activities of human life that need to be washed away, flushed away, dried away, powdered away, forgotten away.

To return now to the room. I mentioned certain things in that room but I left out a lot. I did not speak of the rusty bars on the one small window or what you could see through those bars. I have not spoken of the walls of this room except that one detail was important. On one of the walls of this room, hanging on a nail, was a calendar.

The calendar might partly explain the expression on my wife's face. My wife always sat on the bed and faced the calendar. She never sat on the chair because she felt the chair was for me. After all, I worked in a college and I wrote. I needed the chair and the table to prepare my thoughts which I could lose when actually confronted by my students. I needed the table to correct the work they did and that I dared not think I had taught them. I needed the chair and table to remind me that the use of them, if not their possession, gave me a little status — a feeling that I was not really adrift, but very nearly. But to go back to my wife's face — not really her face so much, as what had happened to it since we had come to this city, is what is important to record. She looked as though the calendar could save her. Nothing but the calendar. Our landlord had a different notion. Listed along with the other items in the room was this item. The list ran thus:

Item : one bed

Item : one mattress

Item : one table

Item : one calendar

It was not goodwill that prompted this frivolous inclusion. It was to remind us of the rent. The date was circled in red. Like a holiday. But my wife saw the calendar as a magical thing, a thing that had powers. One day its power would produce a date that would free her, a date that would release her, a date sometime that would spell "somewhere else". That was her expression. That was her permanent face when I left in the morning and especially when I came back in the evening.

And one day I spoke to her of what I had worked out to balance this unspeakable feeling I had as well. It was in an effort to keep her. It was a move to share, to make her share, to make her speak or speak up or speak out. So.

Look, I said, don't give in; don't just sit there staring at the calendar and thinking of a Champak tree in a court-yard. Or the sound of your mother's voice making *papad* and *achaar*. Or the smell of diyas at Diwali. Just tell yourself there are ways of adjusting to this. To all this. I have found a way.

You have found a way to all this? she said, looking at me in the same way.

Yes. After college I know I have a long way in a train filled, really filled, with bodies hanging or dangling from the overhead straps and looking as though they have been crucified, without the beauty of course — just hanging there till something reminds them that they have reached home. Well, not home but where they have to get off. Now I have found a way to deal with that long, tiring talking-to-no-one journey. I buy twenty paise worth of peanuts at Marine Lines station. And I eat two peanuts at Charni Road and then two more when I reach Grant Road. The trick is that one can't cheat and eat any peanuts between stations. You have to reach a station and....

And, my wife said, till you reach, not home, but where you have to get off?

Yes, I said.

And that helps you to get on with all this?

Yes. And I have another way that sometimes helps.

Yes, tell me if it helps you. And I said,

But also to help you. Perhaps you could find ways to help you adjust to all this.

Yes, tell me, she said again.

If l ever get a seat to sit on in the train I choose a face. And then I look at the face. I look at it for a long time and then I smile. In case.

In case they smile back, she said.

Yes, of course, I said, because then someone will have smiled back.

And when they don't smile back what do you do, what do you feel?

Well, I pretend I hadn't smiled or had thought of something that had made me smile.

I see, she said, you don't feel foolish?

No. Well, not really, and it's worth the risk and, oh well today, when things were really bad I tried something different. I, I —

She waited and so I went on.

Today college was bad. Really bad. I mean nobody seemed to be listening to me in class. I seemed to be talking to myself and there were so many classes and so many people not listening and there was the thought of that long train journey back. So when I got to the telephone booth outside the station I went in and found a number. I mean a telephone number. And I dialled the number to talk to someone.

You mean to anyone. Just talk to someone you didn't know?

Yes, I said. Well, I didn't like the sound of the first voice. It was an irritable voice and I knew it would be no use. So I didn't put the coin in. And I looked up the telephone book again and found a number and dialled. The voice was nice. I liked the voice. So I dropped the coin in and she said, "Who is that speaking?" and I said, "Look, I just want to talk to you if you don't mind and perhaps you might talk to me you know. Just about anything. Just for a while. Of course, if you'd rather not, that's fine. It doesn't matter. I mean I can see that you might not want to," and she said, "I must just turn off the gas. I was cooking the family evening meal." And then when she came back she told me what she was cooking and how the children were already hungry and she asked me if I had any children and what I did. And I said that I was a teacher without any students and a writer without anyone to read what I wrote. She asked me my name and I said I wouldn't be asking her her name and finally she said she would have to get back to the kitchen. I thanked her for being so kind and for talking to me and listening to me. She asked if I would ring her again and I said I didn't know. Then she rang off and I got my peanuts and a seat in my train.

Well, said my wife, which of these methods do you think I should start with to help pass this loneliness, this room, this awful city?

Well, I said and paused. And she prompted.

Peanuts, or the smiling-at-strange faces, or the dialling-of-a-number for a strange voice at the end of a telephone wire?

You might try something else, I said. Try anything. It's bound to help — till all this is over.

And she said, Yes, I'll think of something to help — till all this is over.

Of course, all this was a good twenty years ago and we still live in the same room, and in a city that is now even worse. We have a child. Sometimes the child has the same expression as my wife had when she gazed at the calendar counting the days.

My face, I cannot see — and, and nobody has told me and I dare not ask.

7   *My Ma, Her Ma*

Ba was our maternal grandmother. My mother was only thirteen when she married my father who was fifteen. Technically of course they did not live together till many years later. My mother learnt everything she knew from her mother; she was a wonderful cook and a wonderful wife and mother. She travelled all over India and half of Europe and bore five daughters in as varied places as Sind and Bombay and Hamburg. She was uprooted several times and lived in England and Germany when World War II was on. She managed without my father and in different cities of the world. She managed with little food during rationing and took us down regularly to the air-raid shelters when the dread sirens blew, bore a premature baby weighing two pounds and brought us back to India via Colombo in the last passenger boat from England followed by a torpedo most of the way and with four girls sick to their stomachs. This was our mother from the village of Sojitra. She was a small woman but she was tough. She never learnt to read and write and speak English (on principle) though she understood it very well. She always wore a sari, never ever ate meat or fish or eggs but learnt to cook all of these things first to keep her family well and strong and later because her girls started to like all these alien foods. Later she learnt to live large stretches of her life without my father or with her children far away being educated but she remained the strong backbone of the family always loving, always strict, always remaining true to her worshipful way of life. She ran a great household in her Delhi days with live-in guests from other parts of the world, bringing up five daughters each ready to be as different as possible to shatter any dreams of her own as to how they should be growing up. All her children had long hair which my Ma would oil every Sunday sitting in the sun and when her daughters cut off their hair, it broke her heart. She saw her daughters wear trousers and shorts. She watched her daughters become vets and news readers, she saw her garden filled with dogs, meat was cooked for them in one of the outhouses, she helped my father give parties for soldiers just back from battle with heads bandaged, walking on crutches. She hid Muslims in her home and in the quarters behind the house and watched bravely as the quiet roads outside her home became filled with rabid shouting crowds during Partition. She waited each night till my father returned from the refugee camps, his shirt often covered in blood and filth. My Ma was one of the finest women who lived and what grace she showed under fire! Amazing grace! She retained her fine Indianness no matter how the barbarians battered at her gates, her home and also her greatest beliefs. Through all our illnesses, all five of us, her voice and her hands would be on our foreheads — nursing us through common and uncommon meningitis and jaundice, and measles and chickenpox and mumps and appendicitis, through everything — her hands in iced water sprinkled with Eau de Cologne and one of my father's handkerchiefs right through the night to bring our fevers down. And finally in the mid-50s to watch her world crumbling when there was an auction of so many beloved familiar household things on her beloved lawn! Croquet balls and lamps and mallets, chests and cupboards, chairs and tables. Bravely she packed what was left and made the long journey back to her home grounds left so very long ago — Gujarat. Leaving behind over twenty years of a large beautiful bungalow and a garden that she kept beautiful, rose garden, pillars covered in bridal creeper, shimmering lawns, her kitchen garden with its peas and beans and tomatoes and okra and aubergine. In a small poky house she started all over again. Now it was just my father and my mother. It is ironic that she kept a stray dog called Joey and they adored each other and he was a completely vegetarian dog. As my father started to build a second career in a totally different field my mother also learnt to start from scratch. By now she had fairly severe diabetes, twice she broke her leg and her hip, she got severe migraine headaches and her daughters were scattered — one with a chicken farm in Kihim, one learning to become a cattle-feed expert, one teaching English literature and trying to marry an 'alien' and one working for the airlines, one an actress on the stage and a mother. All this was alien to her; she had wanted her daughters to marry good solid Gujarati boys and have fine children but again disappointment clogged her path. But visits home were filled with love and good food and no recrimination. When she became a grandmother she was greatly loved because she gave so much love.

Gradually, very slowly, my parents built their first and only home. It had some aspects which they had loved in all the houses they had lived in during their long married life together — verandahs, a sunken rose garden, a library, a large swing, a vegetable garden and trees, growing everywhere. Less than a year after they moved in to live in their own home, my mother died with one daughter with her. The dog Joey disappeared never to be found again. He had loved only her. My Ma was sixty-two. My father brought Ba to live in the big house but she was broken by the death of her daughter. And kept disappearing. When people talk of the great changes they have seen in their lifetimes I think always of my Ma who from such a tender age had seen so much from the time she played in her dusty schoolyard, not studying formally after she was twelve years old. How she retained her great love of reading and great films like *Gone with the Wind*. Her favourite actor was Leslie Howard and her favourite film *The Sound of Music*. How does one person live through such events as she did, such cataclysms as she did and remain a thinking, living, independent person? My Ma did. I think she would have loved watching television. She would have loved looking after her garden, her home, her husband and watching her grandchildren grow. And I am now nearly sixty-two and know how young she must have felt to have died at sixty-two.

And my Ba who was my Ma's mother — what did she have in her life except shocks and deaths and loneliness? Well, she was a very spirited, tinier figure even than my Ma and strong and wilful. Outlived all her children but one. Ba is what we called our grandmother. She was fourteen when she was married to an elderly man, a widower with a fifteen-year-old son. My Ba had three more children by the time she was twenty and her elderly husband died by the time she was twenty-five. I was often told when I felt particularly enraged by her life that these marriages worked very well. The 'older' husband being like a father and a husband to his girl-wife. To which I would say she had her own father — also when this older man died she lost both a father and her husband before she was twenty-five, left with an older step-son and three children while she was so young. Then according to the strictest traditions her long hair was shaved off and she had to wear black for her sins and live on the charity of whoever would look after her. Winter and summer, this is what she wore. No chappals on her feet — a thin cotton black sari and blouse. She came often to our home in Delhi. She looked so tiny and so young to be a grand-mother she looked like a sister to our Ma. Except for the black she wore she looked like those graceful Jain nuns who almost run down our filthy streets hardly touching the ground. My Ba glided across the sharp gravel and the green lawns just like that. She had a small black tin trunk with a couple of black saris and blouses and a durrie to sleep on and two cooking vessels. She slept on the floor and cooked her own food after first feeding her god. She ate only one meal a day and bathed in the garden, never in a bathroom.

This too was a masterful yet graceful feat stepping out of her wet sari into her dry one, never exposing any nakedness. She was quaint and odd but we loved her and she was very loving to all of us. Every one of her children, except for one, died before she did. Her stepson in far away Africa, her youngest son in a train compartment between stations and my Ma at the age of sixty-two. My Ba became even odder after my Ma's death. She kept running away. She was always found and then she would run away again. All that loneliness, all those years, all of her life, almost, lived as a widow. She had no childhood. I cannot speak for her married life except for bearing all her children and then her long years of widowhood with her children growing up and going away to far away places. Whenever she ran away it was to try and find her childhood home.

She pursued as many places of worship as she could walking long distances. When she came to Delhi she went to Haridwar and to Mathura. Once she jumped clean out of the car not because our car had leather seats but because someone had told her that the driver was Christian. My own marriage, out of the fold, was kept a well-guarded secret and my husband was given the name of Sunil. She always remembered his name. The rest of us often wondered who she was talking about.

Our numerous dogs and what they ate was another family secret. She would never have come back to our home if she thought we gave them meat. They had to be fed far from home and accepted this cheerfully. She could not understand short hair, wearing shorts and trousers. So many things were kept literally under wraps when she came to stay. She could not understand why we were all not married. She told my Ma in a very agitated manner that it was already too late for at least three out of the five. She fasted once a week for her husband and once a week so that my Ma would have a son. This, added to her one meal a day, made her get thinner and thinner. We loved her and accepted all her dislikes and follies. When her dearest child, my Ma died, she gave up for the first time. She tried starving and wearing cotton in the coldest of Gujarat winters and of course stepped up her disappearing acts like the "walkabouts" of the Australian Abos. It was very sad. She was looking for her own house in the village of Sojitra but it no longer belonged to the family. The car would follow her keeping just out of sight and we would see this tiny figure walking down the road in black, the only colour we had ever seen her wear and when she was tired she would rest by the side of the road or just lie down and go to sleep with her black bundle under her head. Then we would pick her up — she was lighter than a child of three — and drive back home. When these "walkabouts" became impossible my father arranged for her to go back to her village to relative strangers who allowed her to live with them. And she did until she was found asleep, quite dead, quite finally asleep with her cooking vessels and her change of sari and a photograph of my mother.

I think often of her life and the life of my Ma and of our lives. How far they travelled actually and in terms of the changes they suffered. How traditional they were in an India that changed so much. How much I have lost and how much I hate change. What hardship they knew, what they accepted, what they tolerated and how they lived in grace and how very different their lives could have been.

8 *Growing Up*

All of us have caused harm to somebody. Often without realizing it. Often not meaning to. I have committed two deaths. I used to call it murders till my father made me feel less criminal by saying, "Deaths, not murders. Murders are something planned and carried out." So, I'm not off the hook, of course, but murder is out. I do not feel much relief though.

The first was when I was just a girl about ten or eleven. I am now in my sixties but the reminder of one of the deaths is with me always because the sadness of a wasted life stays with one always and because I am faced by that wasted life every time I go home to the small town where I grew up.

Vithal was a family servant. I was extremely fond of him. He was a small, slim, neat, little man with masses of black hair. He would play ball with me. He taught me to climb trees and taught me to cycle. I learnt to ride on his cycle before I got one of my own on my twelfth birthday. He was very patient, running after the cycle, guiding me while I wobbled about. He was most pleased the day I could cycle on my own. He taught me to stop when I wanted to. He taught me how to cycle backwards. I became an expert. If disaster had not struck, I am sure he would have taught me how to drive my father's Ford

V8. But that was not to be. I think Vithal must have been about twenty years old at that time.

One morning I was doing my homework in my favourite room — the library. I was bored. I was looking through books and a photograph dropped out of a book. It was a photograph of two people, one a beautiful woman with quite a lot of jewellery and the other a man with a moustache, handsome and big. He was staring at the woman and had his arm around her shoulders. I felt I had seen the woman somewhere but I could not place her. The handsome man I had never seen. I couldn't find my mother, so I went looking for Vithal. He was my friend. I used to take nearly all my problems or queries to him. He was ironing in a small cubbyhole off the kitchen and he stopped, turned off the switch and took the photograph from me and looked at it. What happened to Vithal's face I shall never forget. Have not to this day. First he let out a moan. Then it was a terrible sound and his face — he'd looked and then closed his eyes for what seemed a long time to me. I didn't know what I had done, but I knew I had done something terrible and that nothing would ever be the same again. I ran after him but he got on to his cycle and tore down the driveway out on to the road.

At lunch he was not there to serve us but I did not say a word about what I had done. Around three that afternoon with everyone resting, the police brought Vithal to my father. He was handcuffed and his face and shirt were spattered with blood and mud. Vithal was crying and repeating something over and over. Then they took him away but I ran after them calling out, "Why, where are they taking you? What has happened?" But he only looked at me and said, "It is hot, go back to the house, the sun is too hot for you," and then they drove away. I think my childhood ended that afternoon. My mother was distraught, crying and would not tell me anything. I went to my father. He said that our Vithal was going to jail for something he had done and that was all. I trailed to the servants' quarters — there was much talk and I asked. I was told that Vithal had killed his wife with a grinding stone — "But why, why?" I kept asking. "She loved someone else and Vithal found out." But how did he find out, I asked knowing what the answer would be. They said, "Vithal found out from a photograph, he found a photograph of the two of them." I went back to the house and locked myself into the bathroom and I cried for Vithal. I cried for myself most bitterly. I cried because now everything would change, nothing would *now* be the same. I had caused this terrible thing with my curiosity about the photograph. I had found the photograph. I had shown it to Vithal. I expected the police to come for me. I fell ill with a high fever and I never told anyone about the photograph. And things did change. I went to school and then on to college. I came back home after a very long time. My father had written to tell me that Vithal was back and how pleased I would be to see him again. He had been set free from jail for good behaviour. He was almost as good as new and back home. "My clothes are ironed as they used to be," my father said, "nobody can iron like Vithal. He is waiting for you to come when you have your holidays." For a long while I did not go home. I was afraid.

After my parents died I went home once a year and missed them unbearably. We who were left would gather and talk of old times, our cousins would come and we would all talk of times long gone sitting in the garden with the trees. When Vithal was not around we often spoke of his remarkable life. One of my cousins said that Vithal's wife used to work for his mother and she was his first love — "More beautiful to a young lad than any film star could ever be, she seemed to glide about the house, her *payals* making a wonderful sound on the stone floors. She would look at me through slightly hooded eyes with a small smile on her lips, very sexy" he said, "my first encounter with a really sexy woman." Another cousin said he was at the trial when my father spoke for Vithal before the final summing up. He spoke of Vithal's character and loyalty and said finally that for such a mild man to have done what he did was because he loved his wife; it was a "crime passional". Vithal was not a violent man. His love was dishonoured. They must *not* give him a life sentence; compassion and mercy should prevail. Vithal got twenty years but he served fifteen because he was so good in jail. When he came out he was fifteen years older with grey in his black hair.

He made home feel home as best he could. He tried to keep up all the ways of my parents saying they had given him a second life. If only he could bring them back, for me, for him. As the shadows lengthened on the lawn the talk would turn to the photograph. Everyone still wondered about the sequence of events. How the photograph could have been in our house and who had shown it to Vithal. It was thought that perhaps someone gave it to my mother and she realizing the implications hid it in a book not thinking anyone would come across it. At this point I always became really agitated and would leave the group, guilty. Why did I show it to Vithal? Not guilty, Vithal was my friend. I really wanted to know. It was curiosity. I was a child. I was guilty, I had caused the death of his wife and a large part of Vithal's life. But though I had ruined his life, removed fifteen years of it, he still calls me "Baby" when I go home though I am in the prime of my life. And only he and I know the secret of the photograph.

All about Avo

Every three weeks (if we were lucky), or every ten days we'd be solemnly interviewing nurses sent by "Miss De Souza's Trained Nurses Association". Later, much later we began to stop interviewing ourselves, we had begun to trust Miss De Souza's judgement entirely. Every time Avo threw a fork or a plate or broke a nurse's chain by just clutching and pulling till it broke, a nurse would leave, even though the pay was so good. "It's the humiliation," some said, others less given to wistful lyricism, said, "She's violent. She'll draw blood next." In the second year of Avo's illness the nurses began to look vaguely familiar, then not so vague and then we realized that even Miss De Souza's Association had reached a point where things had come full circle as with principals in my old college who got their second term because there weren't enough priests to go round. By then, of course, Avo was much more gentle. There's not much you can do with plastic and rubber and melamine, and all the nurses now took off their finery as they stepped into Avo's flat so chains and *mangalsutras* and dangling earrings were only resumed after hours when boyfriends, friends, husbands, sons, sons-in-law and so on came to fetch them. "Who can trust these dark streets?" they said ominously, peering out at almost daylight-glaring neon lights newly installed by a corporation chief. Some said Big Dada had won Ward 5 elections that year. His slogan had won all hearts at the time, "Promises to turn nite into day — only voatpor me." But to get back to first things first, we were all exhausted, our nights and days were all the same in spite of the neon lights because very few of these nurses turned out to be stout of heart; of limb we have already touched on. They had learnt to dial our telephone number shamelessly. At all hours we would hear at the other end a voice saying, "Mother serious, come immediately, no telling what may happen." Sometimes groans and little screams to add a touch of authenticity. Things had to change, we were told, "Wise up, one nurse and one *bai* for the day, and two *bais* at night. Only one of whom should know how to use the telephone if there is an emergency." This worked wonders. All three slept heavily all night because two of the *bais* worked a day shift as well, and Avo needed something to help her to deal with her overactive day. So now into her third year of this strange illness we realized that hers was not an extreme case. Medically it was termed (enigmatically we felt) "long term with many changes up and down."

And such small beginnings. Really small, we said softly. Even we could not hear ourselves say this, and sadly. In all this intense activity the sadness of it. A little fall. That is all.

Not a bad fall. Of this we were certain because after the fall she'd gone to the phone and told her sons. Then separately her two daughters-in-law, and her best friend Elsa and Mr. Everiste De Gama, not Mrs. De Gama who had answered the phone. All these people had been told it was just a little fall, not to worry and not to tell anyone. All these people being simple and loyal and loving, rushed to Avo. They found her holding court, in the blouse and petticoat she had fallen in. Those listening in various attitudes of enthralment, interest, boredom, and so on were the two ladies from the next flat, the sweeper, the *dhobi*, the *mali*, the lift No.1 man and two small children Anu and Sonu from the third floor who were always happier on the eighth floor because their mother was given to slapping her children in the mornings and calling out the while, "why have children, why marry, it is a curse." Sonu and Anu repeated this in all their singing and chanting games and were at the moment doing this as they skipped to a rope, "why marry (skip skip), why have children (skip skip) it is a curse (skip skip) repeat, it is a curse." The parish priest who had just nipped over thinking it was Sunday and there might be a spot of port wine going was shocked. "Heathen children," he muttered and they incorporated him in their skipping game, "Good morning, Father, to you (skip) Father good morning (skip)." Truly touched, the good Father said, "Good morning, and bless you children," thinking, "they probably go to a good Catholic school". He ignored their receding voices which sang out, "girly, girly father, (skip) wearing girly skirts (skip)". He addressed himself to Avo firmly. "What seems to be the matter here?"

"I fell Father, Father I have fallen down." Gravely he said "There, there, no one falls so low or so badly that they cannot rise." But now all that was past, she had moved into yet another phase — her eating needs, appetites, became stranger and odder — potato wafers propped up on part of her pillow, little bits of cold tongue and chocolate. Only milk chocolate, only Cadbury's, sometimes Amul, and then she moved into a phase of lemon sweets, not orange not pink or red sweets, only lemon. In despair, eggs put into her coffee (ugh) or sustaining soups fortified with an egg were made carefully and on a good day found the feeder and the fed struggling as with death, or on a bad day just draped over the feeder or the aforesaid pillow. The wise ones, there are always so many when someone is ill, "know-alls" by any other name, would whisper, "she should have a few more scans and things. You never know (whisper whisper) how can she not eat!"

"No more scans and things," we said. "She has had them all. Go away, you lot just go away!" They did and spread the word being good souls and caring in their own way. They are just starving her, really. Good lord! you don't mean actually starving. Yes, yes just lemon sweets as many as she wants and occasionally a plastic bowl of chips, no not even chips, wafers, really you know, nibbles at a child's birthday party for ever so long. Shock, amazement, you will realize the mean bit of accuracy "plastic bowl" added just the right touch of authenticity. They had all seen and known proud cupboards full of the very finest Chinese, German, French and even English dinner sets for fifteen, and tea and coffee sets for eight and these "mean captors" now fed mean tidbits out of plastic. "Hard or soft?" they asked. The plastic, they meant. The answers were given. Horror all round. "Dear God," they prayed, "fate worse than death to fall ill and have only one's family around, dear God save us from this. Give us always strangers if we fall ill, only strangers at our bedsides." After the short prayer, they said, "Well

now who will break it to Father D'Costa, I can't this
Sunday and it shouldn't wait till next. Shall we go across
ourselves now? I mean, a sort of little morning visit. He
ought to be told, he might like to weave something into
his sermon. He's anyway the quickest way to get this
news around the parish. It won't look right if we, you
know, if we were the ones to speak first, poor, poor, friend
of our childhood."

The visit to Father D' Costa was not a success. "Our
sister Avo is in the best possible hands. I go there every
Sunday after mass and give her Communion and it is true
she will not eat properly. Even when I sit with her and
the family she will only nibble potato wafers with
chocolate — Cadbury's preferably and lemon sweets. But
the doctor has been there many a Sunday and says it is
all right. She will find her level soon — at the moment
this is her level — and now dear ladies of my parish if
you are not too busy, I have many duties to finish. Good
morning." He was not the fool he looked or gave out to
be. Snubbed they were but started immediately working
on some way to remove him — they had often removed
parish priests in the past. A formidable lot. But that really
is another story. For now we may allow ourselves only a
quiet, "Hurray for Pooh, or rather Father D' Costa."

To return to our other difficulties. Avo refused to get
out of bed — absolutely. Lifted bodily for her daily bath
and what books call politely ablutions, that was it. She
would not even sit up. "Lovely wheelchair. Beautiful
wheelchair, and into the lift and then into the car for a
lovely drive — think, Avo just think of it," we tempted.

"No," she said, "I will not and you cannot make me."
It was true. We could not. Make her do anything she

decided she would not do. We were weak and she was strong. Long ago nursery-cum hymn-cum-prayer for small children returned to our minds. "Jesus loves me, this I know, for the Bible tells me so. Little ones to Him belong we are weak but He is strong, yes Jesus loves me (repeat) yes Jesus loves me (repeat), Yes, Jesus loves me, the Bible tells me so." Now why does that dreadful little song haunt me, us. Ah yes, the refrain, "We are weak and she is STRONG."

The next phase. Shocking the visitors further. Forgetting (the right things) and remembering (the wrong) it is called. Avo receiving visitors. "And when are you getting married, finally?" This to someone visiting bringing husband, child, grandchild in tow.

Or long ago love affairs or suicides were mentioned or spoken about; visits became difficult, gradually, slowly, hardly anyone visited. Sometimes people telephoned but heard things at the other the end of the line like, "Who, who? I don't know anyone of that name," or worse. Finally it came down to Father D'Costa, the two nurses, the two *bais*, the doctor, the physiotherapist and the family. Of this lot the physiotherapist gave up first. Stout of heart and limb herself, she said, "I'm not coming any more — it's just wasting your money and I can't bear to face this terrible failure — she won't walk, she's given up, there are those who do and those that won't, and she won't. That's all there is to it."

And she left. Avo called out, "Goodbye and don't forget, take the walking stick and the trainer and the walker and the wheelchair. I won't be needing those, will I?" Suddenly her room was just a bed. And on that bed a pillow and under that pillow a pair of chappals. And of course Avo. On that day this triumph of hers was an even greater victory than the — not-eating-anything-but-wafers-tongue-and-chocolate-and lemon sweets. This was on another scale altogether.

Now the chappals under her pillow took her on strange journeys. The house where she was born, the home she grew up in, her old school, her boarding school, her holidays, her husband's home, their married home, the children's home. Their first communion, their school, their college, their going away, their coming back, their girlfriends, her husband's extraordinary ability on the dance floor, "Oh, Robert could dance divinely, even on skates — Oh, those were dances on Saturday nights! Robert was always much in demand." And of course there was no logic to it. One memory of a dance, the next why she would never wear mauve or purple, the next a sanitorium in Panchgani, a house for a holiday, a church, first communion, the two little boys on the same day. Quick as lightning, delighted, we would hand her a photograph — large, sepia stained but happily arranged seated grown-ups and a priest. Two little boys in white and bow ties, "Look, Avo, look, there it is."

"Don't shout, I'm not deaf," and Avo turned her face away — "Not now, not now," she said, "then was then." The burden now too great to face of such a long ago yesterday. Abashed we hid the faded happy day.

Another day, mind clear she said, "Call Delmira, where is she, tell her the dining-room roof is leaking again, call her, I will tell her myself." Pandemonium — who is Delmira? What is she? and then "Whiskers. you'll find him drunk behind the soup cauldron." After ringing, hunting, looking up, short of holding seances Delmira was discovered to have been a servant fifty years ago. One day calling for an aunt who was a nursing nun — "Call her I loved her call her." And then, "Darling girl don't wear mauve it means a death. If I'd had a daughter I would have called her Eugenia, she would have been beautiful like my mother, or there was a beautiful staircase at Villa D'Este, let's go there, let's go there now. To the big house, now. But don't wear mauve, darling it means death."

"I had a friend called Sunita, did you know her? I had a friend called Molly, do you know Molly? Do you know Elsa, and Margie? and Sylvia who lives in Lisbon? In Panjim she was my best friend. She can't hear very well now. Not deaf though." This was her startling talk, day after day.

Then she got much better perhaps because finally Miss D'Souza's setup had sent someone called Margaret. Large, friendly, smiling Margaret. Looked like every- body's Mum, a lovely Mum. She coaxed, persuaded, bullied, cajoled Avo by turns and sometimes all these things at the same time and made Avo eat. No more awful potato wafers, and lemon sweets and milk chocolate. Real food. Miraculous khichdi. Boiled vegetables. A bit of fruit. Avo got better. She recognized us. She interrupted more — she did not allow private conversations. She also got angry a lot more. She sang snatches of old remem- bered songs. She spoke of her father a great deal. She repeated over and over something her father had said, she spoke of her mother's great beauty. She never got out of bed. Wonderful Margaret could make her do so many things but this, this one thing she could not do. No wheelchair. No getting out of bed. And that really was that. And then one day, without the least warning Avo had another stroke. A mighty one. A bad one. Now she could not move. Except the one hand — it moved and it moved and it was trying to tell us something, trying to show us something. This hand in the still room wove patterns that we could not understand. And we tried to understand, and we tried to guess, and the hand moved and moved and it was the saddest thing of all the things that we had seen for twenty-four months and add another six. And we wished that she would ask for lemon sweets, or tongue or those awful potato wafers or Cadbury milk chocolate, and we wished she would be rude or call us by the wrong names or throw down a cup of soup on a newly changed sheet, we wished she would ask for a weak drink of whisky with water. Anything. Just anything. But she couldn't and didn't. In the still room with the bed in the centre, a hand moved and was still and then moved again. On the sixth day Avo died.

The funeral was another mess altogether — John Pinto, undertakers, established 1908, went to the wrong address and finally arrived when all the mourners looked half-dead having had to mourn for so long in a small room with Avo peaceful on ice and a slow fan turning and the candles flickering. Then the lift packed in and the coffin could hardly make it down the eight storeys. Finally, we got it into the hearse as the evening post brought a letter and a "get well" card for Avo.

Haines road cemetery at last and an immaculate great grandson of John Pinto (undertakers, established 1908) straightened the crooked cross and had a wreath of his own as Avo was lowered into the open grave. And the sun went down.

The wake was cheerful. Lots to drink and eat, a party

Avo would have enjoyed greatly. And so the long chapter ended. The priest from the chapel across from Avo's asked when we would like Avo's piano returned — she had generously let them use it for fifteen years. We felt mean asking for it back. So Avo's piano is still in the chapel across from Avo's and you can hear it at the evening service on Sundays.

And as I said before some things have such small beginnings. Really small. Sometimes over the coming months we would think this or say it in hushed whispers. And sadly. It is very important to say because there is so much activity and attendant business, circumstances to a long illness that often it is easy to forget how sad it all was. A little fall. That is all.

10 Smoke Gets in Your Eyes

Anjali had slaved away a whole day, two days really and today was the birthday bash to end all bashes. It was Ram's sixty-fifth birthday. All his old friends and buddies, some half a century old. Anjali hated parties and had been firm over thirty-five years of marriage but this year was special, time was passing, she had given in. There was to be singing and a large cake and the house had to look spectacular. But she hated parties, specially her own; she worried about everything and never had a good time and always seemed to get her migraine attacks bang in the middle of one of them. So many things could go wrong. The ice would be late, the guests would be late or too early, the lights would fuse, the fridge would conk out, the dog would bite one of the guests, the food would be awful, all kinds of disasters. The party would be boring and everyone would go home early. As Anjali thought these thoughts she polished the brass and the silver, tucked away all sorts of unseemly things under the beds, brought out the best counterpanes, covered the cushions with fresh cushion covers, counted the cutlery. No one could have both a fork and a spoon. Just one of either. Thirty-five people, where would they sit? Where would they stand? Anyway, they could only have a fork or a spoon. Anjali had never had such a large party. How did other people do it? She hoped the borrowed waiter would come on time. Find the house. Take off the purple name-tag from his uniform. Now she started on the plates. She was all right with plates. Thirty really good plates. The family must use the chipped ones in daily use. She was secretly pleased that fourteen people could not come. Now count the napkins and start on the glasses. Twenty-five firm whisky people, five wine or soft drink people and the rest beer or vodka. No Bloody Marys, no last minute can openers for the tomato juice tins and no red stains all over the best tablecloths. Please let Perfect Ice find the house and be on time.

This was the first day in sixty days that she hadn't gone to the hospital. She knew that nobody's life depended on her but she felt guilty and worried. They had started a new story yesterday and perhaps he would fret wanting to know how the story would end. Anyway she'd be going tomorrow. She wanted to see his pale bearded face on the pillow. Would his eyes be open wide or would they be exhausted and seem to stare at nothing, would it be a good day for him or would it be wretched, would he say her name or would he turn away not wanting anyone? Stop thinking, just get on with the things you have to do. She went to the kitchen. Thomas was chopping onions and garlic and humming. He was in his element. He loved dinner parties, he could use all the oil he wanted, all the masalas. He could cook pork and fry *puris* and make enough *pullao* for sixty. He went on humming and thought of the praise he would get later that night. This was the life, he seemed to be humming, also he seemed to be telling me to get on with all the light work. So Anjali got on with the less important work, dusting and tidying the three rooms and the terrace. Worrying. It better not rain tonight. Yesterday there had been a real downpour. Thunder and lightning and sheets of rain and this was the end of October. Tonight it would ruin everything. Certain windows would have to be closed, the pianist would have to be indoors. Nobody would see her miniature rain forest, her orchids, her wild orchids in a pot, leaves turned red. It must not rain. Please God.

She thought of the hospital and the hospital bed and smell of disinfectant, and the corridors and sixty days. He'd been in there for so long and how he must long for home and his own bed and his books and the familiar prints on the walls! Sixty days. He would have come to this party, he would have been with them tonight. Kamla had promised to come, even if it was just for a drink. On the phone this morning she had said, "It will cheer me up, God knows I need cheering up, I"ll meet all the old friends, I'm taking a sari to change into and when the day nurse hands over to the night nurse, you'll see me."

By now the three rooms looked rather nice and she moved to her small terrace. This was her favourite place in all the house. She watered the trees and the orchids, blessed them for being in bloom and then considered where the pianist would sit, perhaps in this corner and the white rocking horse could be under the bamboo. A couple of cane stools and it would be perfect. That is if it did not rain. Now she would rest. But first ring the hospital, "Nursing Home please, yes Room 18. Minnie, this is Anjali. How is he? Oh good, very good, I am glad, no, I can't come today. It's Ram's birthday, but I'll be there tomorrow same time. Give him lots of love and to Kamla." She lay down and closed her eyes. In all their thirty-five years together she had never let Ram have a birthday bash. He was a gregarious person and loved his friends and a jolly drink and a sing song. Now he was sixty-five. When did we stop being young, when did we grow old and older? How did it happen? When? Was it because of or in spite of us? After a while she got up and it was evening. Now the house looked even better with the lamps on. You couldn't see the rough edges of dust or cobweb. The paintings looked luminous, the glasses shone, the wood looked polished and the leaves on the terrace shone and gleamed as in a red forest. The pianist arrived and settled down in his corner with his plugs and wires and speaker. Ram came home and bathed and settled down for a short snooze. Perfect ice came on time. The starters were safely in the oven. The cake in the fridge. The smell of food wafting through the house. Anjali changed and tried to look nice. It was taking longer and longer to look even reasonably nice these days.

The first guests started arriving. Wonderful parcels and gifts with green and blue and red wrapping paper, ribbon and tinsel stars everywhere. The pianist played happy songs and people sang and danced together to 'Pretty Woman', 'Walking My Baby Back Home', 'That's My Gal', 'Chatanuga Chu Chu', 'On The Sunny Side of The Street' and gradually the mood grew mellow and sadder and the pianist played sad nostalgic songs — 'And the autumn weather turns the leaves to flame and I haven't got time for the waiting game' — and when he played 'Smoke Gets in Your Eyes' — everyone sang and eyes filled with tears as though the words were their lives — now laughing friends deride, tears I cannot hide, so

I smile and say, when a lovely flame dies 'Smoke gets in your eyes.'

Anjali rang the bell loud and firm, "Dinner's on, come and get it." Laughing and joking and jostling each other they came downstairs for dinner. The dinner was good and they sang lustily when the cake came in flaming with candles. Then the early leavers left but many stayed behind hugging their cherry brandys and their cocoa. It was safe here with memories, with old friends — outside lay a hostile world; here the lamps were low and the cushions deep and soft. Reminiscing time. Fifty years of friendship time — recalling school and pretty teachers, girlfriends, being good or bad at sports, time and long ago times, college times and bunking lectures and serious girl friends and doing plays "Oh remember the time you forgot your entrance and I covered for you for ten minutes, and remember that other time" laughing and old jokes, what they were and what they felt and now all nearly over sixty, as old as their parents had once been and now? And now it was past one in the morning and the plates cleared and put away, the borrowed waiter gone by the last bus. The door burst open and Kamla was in the room in a blood red sari. She stood in the doorway and her face was like Medea's when Jason betrayed her; and when they reached her to hug and hold her, they knew she didn't have to say it because they could hear the words before they were spoken, "Oh he's gone, he's really gone, finally gone. He would have been sixty in January he was the youngest of us all, and he's grown up and he's gone. All he said was, 'I'm going, I'm so tired' and I kissed his hands and his face and turned down the light and closed the door behind me and walked down that corridor and I've come here because I wanted to come. I was looking forward to this reunion, this party. I chose this sari this morning and I told him I was going to be with you this evening, this night to greet you and all the friends of our youth." Ram gave her a large brandy and we put her to bed. We drove to the hospital and went up to Room 18. It was true. Just as she had said. He was gone. He lay as if asleep after a long and weary battle.

Anjali felt so sad and spent and picked up the book she had brought with the book-marker between the pages where they had stopped reading saying, "Tomorrow we'll finish the story." Now he would never hear the end of the story. He had only known part of the story. And she thought, what's it all for? Why do we build relationships and companionship and love and celebrate each passing day and year? This is how it really ends. This is what it really is all about. A lonely face on a white pillow. We grow closer and closer to this. This is why we have birthday parties. To stave off the last hour — to ignore the dark at the top of the stairs. The dark at the bend of the road. Early that morning she had tied a garland of fresh Indian marigolds over the front door for her husband's sixty-fifth year under heaven. And now there was a death in the family. And all their friends of the night would remember and be afraid for the turn of the door knob, for the telegram late at night and the sound of the telephone too early in the morning. Now they would keep looking into the future as a place of shadows and darkness.

But a few days after the funeral and the useless, necessary things we said about the passing of grief we went away to Uran.

We played tennis on the court by the sea and watched two little girls play riding on their red cycles calling out "Dadda John, Dadda John look at me," and in the evening we watched a great ball of fire sink into the black water and we raised our glasses under the dark still casuarinas and said, "To absent friends."

11   *Islands in the River*

Off for the weekend. Pack only shorts and T-shirts and sandals, a book, toiletry, medicines and fun things for the birthday and Easter wine and cake. Off for a long weekend — a friend's birthday, Easter week and close long-time friends.

Wake extra early, water the plants, kiss dog watching with sad eyes, pack and load the car and water for the journey. Last minute drill — check geysers, the T.V., the A.C., the toaster and solemnly promise no quarrels. No raised voices, keep to safe topics, our children, books, film, plays, gentle gossip, nothing malicious. No politics, no religion. And remember this time I shall raise the birthday toast. "Friendship, Peace, Love." Off then past the heavier aggressive traffic, all the cars in Bombay leaving for the long weekend — cars packed with children, babies, teddybears, loud music playing *"choli ke peechay"* past all this, past the earlier heavy traffic and stop at the beginning of the main ghat. Favourite restaurant "Happy Home" for *batata vada* and chutney, coffee and clean loo. Settling down to delicious vadas and bad but hot coffee. Next to us a young, noisy, excited family with two little girls in pink T-shirts and shorts eating tomato ketchup and chips and pointing to their obviously new jeep trendily painted to resemble jungle camouflage a small tank. They couldn't wait to be off. Neither could we. Up and up the ghats past huge hoardings for impossible resorts with swimming pools and casinos and romantic cafes. Past Lonavala and Khandala and down to Talegaon. Gentle hills, little cottages nestled between plateaux rocks and trees. No loud sounds of traffic. Only bees humming in the sun and far away a water wheel being worked. No traffic, only a woman with her shopping, a boy on his new cycle. A cat or two. Everything bone dry waiting for rain. The landscape must change dramatically when the rains come. Everything must be green and mists must rise from these hills and plateaux with far away sounds of waterfalls. Dry gardens but many flowering trees and two large old *champak* trees dropping pink and white flowers even as we passed.

What must it be like during the rains? It could easily become Wuthering Heights' country — the stark hills and plateaux, black rocks becoming lush green with the rains and mist rising out of the dark valleys and small purple flowers bursting out of these dry straw-coloured spiky shrubs. Yes, it was stark enough. Rolling, gentle, downhill now all the way.

Arrive in Poona. A hot dusty drive, past hot dusty old houses set in large dusty gardens and old dusty trees over a bridge. Then gradually past shadier streets and less dusty-looking houses with green lawns and sprinklers and massed orange and pink bougainvilleas. Then the dreaded Osho country with guarded black fencing and black walls and black granite, what are they fencing out or fencing in, all the many reds ever seen from the darkest prune red to the lightest, and couples holding hands or linking arms, talking or just walking and sitting and smoking, this palette of reds everywhere against their chosen black. Past all that, even walls covered with their gowns and dresses and swimsuits all red hanging on hangers sold from walls.

Arrived at our destination. Warmth and greetings and admiration for a new home with a river all to themselves. Their view was river. Not a rushing, gushing, brown thing but a river to dream by and read by and write by and look at all day long. To find peace by blue-green over white rocks and water hyacinths with flecks of mauve and three white birds wheeling in the sky above. A family of speckled ducklings busy bobbing up and down in a duck's way. On the opposite bank trees and shrubs and far away, imagined Jeddah-like white dwellings. Many boozy hours later and several toasts to "Friendship, Peace and love." Off for a week- end afternoon snooze. Sounds of birds and the louder sound of the desert cooler. The long weekend truly begins.

Later, afternoon tea in the balcony again, we are river-viewing — the colours have changed; the white rocks now more grey, the ducklings less busy and huddling and bobbing close together and effortlessly in darker wine waters. Peace. Blessed peace. No sounds. High up a white bird. Poised.

Late evening, the ritual for mosquito time. Close and lock the netting doors, draw the heavy curtains, switch on the mosquito mats, rub Odomos or Auten on bits of skin showing. Off with shorts, on with trousers. Eve of Easter go to an old, old Anglican church to hear a choral Easter cantata. Old church, no statues, huge brass plaques on the walls telling of the sad "death of Kings", great white pillars and old fans with only two wings endlessly

turning and as the voices soared, the mosquitoes came
into their own, lots of legs to bite, "pass the Odomos",
quick, frenzied scratching, blood flowing as a beautiful
voice sang "they have taken away my Lord and I know
not where they have laid him." Afterwards, the moon
hanging low in the sky and the smell of air scented with
flowers. Back to the flat with its own river dark now and
quiet waiting for morning. Easter Sunday and the storm
broke over hot cross buns and toast and marmalade.
Unbelievably the storm broke not over Religion or Politics
but over a new bakery called Just Baked; a small quarrel
began and grew and grew till it was all wrecked, finished,
the peace, the river and its islands, its white birds and
water hyacinths and the small ducklings. All shattered,
broken, things said which could not be unsaid. How could
a place so near a healing river have had these vibrations,
a little quarrel becoming a great storm? Old, tested, tried,
old friends and on Easter Sunday. How? But in minutes
everything hanging out as they say — things remembered
buried for ages, all coming out. The past is so long. None
of the good things, the good times remained. Everything
gone. Friendships, peace, love gone with the wind. Now
only words like bullets, harsh words, harsh memories,
raised. Voices, doors banged and outside the window, the
river flowed on peacefully and the white bird lifted itself
up over the water and into the sky.

Nothing left to do. All in shambles. Go to the spare
room, collect one's things, check the cupboard, the hook
behind the bathroom door. Pack and leave. Now the cases
in the hall. Jijabai cleaning the floors looks up startled as
we leave. She had heard the raised voices, wondered why
things were so noisy — only yesterday it had been so

friendly, so companionable. They had included her in their smiles and happiness and warmth. Yesterday they were reading on coming back from a swim with a large red towel, a small fashion show with dark red Oshu gowns. Jijabai bent her head again and carried on. Three rooms left to do.

To the station to get a taxi and then four hours of dust and heat and diesel fumes and smell of fresh tar and many, many upturned, overturned, bashed and crashed lorries and cars. All journeys are like this. The way out full of expectation and clean clothes and excitement — what to do and what to say to the dear familiar faces — the *batata vadas*. Talegaon waiting for rain, the flowering trees, the dry earth and hills. And then the love and friendship. And the journey back. Harsh voices and slammed doors and clothes not folded but flung into suitcases and the whole world turned upside down, the world of "telegrams and anger". And yet the river had been there flowing gently with its white rocks and the white birds wheeling in a blue sky. Perhaps it was really because of the precious wine glass that had shattered the night before. A tall stemmed beautiful glass. Knocked over and broken, shattering God knows what other memories, when bought or given as a token of love, drunk from, raised delicately a toast, "Friendship, Peace, Love" but here knocked over. The fragility of glass and beautiful things and friendships. All too fragile glass and friendship. Strong bonds are weak, long marriages, loving friendships, a small slip, a nagging word one too often, teeth set on edge, over the edge, in one moment of time. Truly "things fall apart, the centre cannot hold" as time moves on, cannot contain faith and religion and man and boundaries and frontiers. Marriages and friendships. Fragile. Glass with Care. This side up. One careless gesture the glass breaks, one careless remark and total collapse of a stout party.

At the last bend of the ghats, the very last, we pulled up suddenly. A familiar jeep camouflaged, the children's choice. Twisted unrecognized metal. Was this a car? Couldn't tell which was the front, which the back. One seat flung clean across the road, a bent plastic water bottle and bit of a T-shirt waving from a bush, pink. How happy they had been, how happy they had looked, tomato ketchup and chips. What were they thinking just before the fatal moment, awful to contemplate — all our lives in a stranger's hand. "Please let us arrive home safely. Powers that are and be, hover over us."

"Dear God, let them not have known, let them all have died together and at once."

So, shocked and saddened, we sat by the rockside and listened to the silence between the traffic sounds. And then we left that benighted place. When we got back we dialled the Pune number and said to the answering machine "Friendship, Peace, Love" and believed we heard the river in the background and imagined the white rocks and the blue-green water and the water hyacinths and the white bird climbing into the blue sky.

12 Lies, Lies and Letters Instead

Alia learnt letter-writing in school with the nuns. The nuns taught her what a letter should be rather than what it could be. Saturday morning was letter-writing day. Rubbers were essential for rubbing out what she wrote and for the changes made — "I miss you very, very much." The nuns said, "No need for that. Just say, I am well, I hope you are well." If she wrote, "The nuns are cruel they make me eat meat", she was told, "Now rub that out and write — 'the nuns are teaching me how to be a good girl and eat up everything on my plate'." The nuns taught Alia that lies are all right in letters. Truth was wrong and must be rubbed off the page. Her parents told her years later that they had guessed how unhappy she had been because the letters seemed smudged with rubber marks and tear marks. Many years later Alia learnt to write her own letters and she always told the truth far better than when she spoke, when she often found she told little white lies — to be polite or not to hurt. But letters were sacred, they had to be the whole truth. Nothing but.

Some people's lives are dominated by letters. Rather, the wonder of their lives open up with letters. What friends say in letters, how incidents are described in letters, how you read the lines and words and between the lines and words, and how everyone writes unique letters. Alia loved to get letters and she laid great store by them. So the early teaching of the nuns about telling lies did not spoil things for her later on. Alia never ate meat again. So much for nuns.

In some families the men get to travel, the women wait. For the postman. Alia's grandmother waited for letters and through letters heard of the splendour of Africa, of the heat and the lions, the waterfalls and the trade in Nairobi and Uganda. She never went to Africa but the village postman brought her letters so she felt she knew it. Alia's mother read of Hamburg and Austria and Paris and London from her letters, so she felt she had been to all those places and seen many things.

And Alia waited for the postman. And she learnt of Brazil and Japan and Geneva and Bangkok from the letters he brought. And later from her dear friends read of the outbacks in Australia and the leaves turning gold in New England in the fall and walking the streets of Broadway and crossing Central Park. She read of old barns and windmills turned into homes in the south of France and of the cobbled streets of Brussels. Truly letters were a great way to travel and learn without actually packing a suitcase.

And then one day Alia found a box of letters hidden away in a cupboard. Her husband's cupboard. She had always liked boxes to hold secrets, collections of shells, stones, feathers, letters.

That is how she found the letters. There were three hundred and sixty-five letters, written in a single year, a rubber band around each month, thirty or thirty-one letters. For February there were twenty-eight. Starting

with the earliest one she read, read them right through
to the end. She cried a great deal. When she had finished
all of them she moaned and rocked, and rocked and
moaned. The letters told a story. A woman from another
town or her own and a name that could be a stranger
or a friend in another guise. She thought of the nuns.
The guise of woman in love, in thrall, in lust. With Alia's
husband. His name was always his name except for some
endearments. The woman's identity remained secret. She
seemed young enough and very literate and fathoms deep
— of course. It was clear that they had met and fallen
in love obsessively and they had gone on meeting at
intervals. Sometimes every week, sometimes a fortnight
or ten days passed. The woman was distracted with grief
when an appointment was missed and she had written
to him every single day of that year. Her husband too
it would seem had written to her very, very often. The
woman longed and hungered for his letters.

Alia suddenly realized just how jealous she was. She
felt terrible, she hadn't felt like this since she was
sixteen and then twenty-one. She was now sixty-two.
This emotion had been long forgotten. She was outraged
at feeling like this. They obviously shared something.
No, they quite obviously shared a great deal. She
remembered how once a very long time ago, she and
her husband had been separated by a continent for over
a year when the child was little. She had written to him
every late evening for that whole year. All days she had
kept very busy with the child with her own work, with
the dog. But late each evening she had made a cup of
coffee and had sat down to write to him. They must
have been boring letters. Not like these that she had

been reading. But she had written of the day's small events, how the child was doing, how the dog was doing, how the plants were growing and how much she missed him, missed him. She had missed him agonizingly and had waited for the postman each day at ten in the morning and at four in the afternoon and had hated Sundays because he would not come. Enough of this. Enough, she thought. I wrote then because I needed to. And this creature, this other woman wrote everyday because she needed to. But what of him? What had he needed, what had he missed so much in her/his wife? What of his letters? Where had he written them and when? He woke up earlier and earlier "older people need less sleep" — "ho hum!" she thought. Or in office, "in slack hours". Older people need less sleep, not less love it would seem. Stop that. Be your age. Spilt milk and all that. Letters aren't reality — perhaps a different reality. Things you cannot or don't say all the time. You work out and write later. You work out everything later, you embroider later, in letters to confirm something done, or something not done or something you wish had happened, or something. But letters were important. They were confirmation. They did make real. They did remind. They did rejuvenate. They did help when things seemed long ago and dusty and dreary and in another country and "besides the wench is dead". Alia pulled up shortly. Of course while I'm maundering on, the wench is dead. This wench in any case. Me. Letters were romance. Letters were past. Letters confirmed how much you were loved, how much you loved. Once, glowingly you might have been loved. Coffee and patties at Pyrk's holding hands. Shit. Letters were a whole

world. you had peopled, filled. And when you felt
unloved, unwanted, unregarded and in corners thrown,
when you were most vulnerable, letters helped. Letters
that said, "I shall love you always and always!" letters
said, "forever and ever", letters said remember that
morning, that afternoon, that evening, that night, that
boat that had, that — letters started extravagantly, "My
very own, my beloved, my dearest dear, my life" —
letters unwind and bind. Letters tell the truth. Especially
if you are shy. Letters ended so permanently they said,
I can't wait till next time. I'm yours forever, all, all my
love and more. Letters were like the land of Elizabeth
and Robert Browning. Letters made you feel part of
poetry, literature, letters made you more beautiful and
desirable, no mirror could show. Now these letters. Alia
read them all, every one of them again. They revealed
the whole truth. No nuns' lies here. They told of love
in her time, in her home, in her bed, as she grew old
in it. She was finished. She had invested everything in
her life. Now these letters.

Alia went to a secret drawer in her desk and took out
her own letters from her husband. They had known each
other forty years or more. Each year's letters bound in
ribbon. She read them all — because she needed by now
to believe that she too had once been greatly loved and
greatly cherished. And then she tore them up, all of them.
She went around the house pinning them to pictures and
paintings, hanging them and sticking them on the staircase, on the bed head, on the mirrors — Everywhere.
After all there were so many of them. Even on the shower
curtain. And when she was finished, she felt she had run
many miles and felt very tired and very sad. Then she sat

down and waited for her husband, her dear love and companion and dearest friend in all the world to come back. For once she had been all to him and he had been all to her. The letters told the truth. The life had been nuns' lies.

13   *Books Last*

Off to the conference. As a spouse. A stopover in Singapore before getting on to another plane to Hong Kong. Ten years ago with her father a similar break of journey at this incredible airport, the dead unreal hour, not day, not night, walking or using the gleaming escalators — a whole hour to gawp and gape at the wonders in the Duty Free shops. Wines and liquors, cigarettes and perfumes and fine dark chocolate. They had walked slowly, she kept tugging his sleeve saying, "Let's go into this one; let's buy some After Eights, let's buy some Bond Street Cologne by Yardley, let's get your favourite Glenlivet, let's —" and her father had said, "Let's just look, let's just enjoy it, we have no real needs, look at the fountain and the orchids, come."

Now ten years on.

Hong Kong and its mountains sweeping down into its seas, its islands, its tall buildings, its star ferry, its boats and yachts, its shops and wonderful shop signs in fiery red and gold in Chinese or English. And in old Macau a very old Taoist Buddhist temple, quiet courtyard with an old tree twisted and gnarled and incense burning. In one room a great laughing Buddha, in another a ferocious terrifying dragon painting on a whole wall, black and grey spewing white smoke. And in another she was pulled up

short. A gay paper house, a large paper bed and everything a man might need made of paper, "old custom when
somebody die, to help man in his new abode", our guide,
"call me Joey please", explained. The custom was exactly
like the one her father had told her about. On the last
day of rituals for the dead, a bed was heaped with all the
necessary things a man would need when he arrived in
his new home. Her father did not want it, it's such a
waste, it's really all for the priests anyway — and she
laughing then had said, "What? Not your spectacles and
your books to read?"

It came back to her in this old, old temple made of
wood as grey as cement, its incense, its still quiet tree in
the courtyard. So now he came to her, her father, as they
walked these streets and up the many steps to Saint Paul's,
to its massive facade like a stage prop, "You can't take
it with you finally, so — enjoy, savour, do not covet, live
free of possessions." He had walked gravely and slowly,
looking at everything and made her feel ashamed of her
excited greed and her repeated cry, "But we must buy
something —" and he had said,

"Why must —?"

And she, "Because it's all here waiting. We may never
be here again." And he, "Why not admire its orderliness,
taste the courtesy of its smiling keepers, why buy anything?"

But she had persisted, "But gifts for the family, for
friends, for ourselves? Now that we are here."

And he said, "No, why covet? Why need to possess?
Just look and be satisfied; as for our friends and relations,
they must like us for ourselves not for the gifts we bring
them."

"But you buy books, you always have," she had said.

And he said, "Books are different, books last. Now let us continue our walk." Soon they were back in the plane. Ten years ago.

Now ten years on she was back in this shoppers' paradise, she looked and she bought, and she bought and looked some more, and soon became insatiable. She found wonderful things and her husband and her son urged her to buy all sorts of necessary — and unnecessary — things. And she watched her son choose things for his new wife, he chose carefully and generously and she thought, my father was wrong, surely, there was much blessing and joy in giving. Her son would turn to her and say, "What do you think, Ma? Do you thinks this pink or this black or both?" And though her breath caught in a sudden pang which she recognized as jealousy she chose for him fairly because she loved her son and her daughter-in-law.

That night she had a dream most real, most terrible in its closeness. She got up and stood looking out of the window at an alien landscape. Her father in all his realness, his own voice said, "Let us walk a little and sit on that white bench under the trees. If you love these trees for their beauty you would not try to remove them. You loved Chartres, the stained glass of St Chapelle, the Fra Angelico's the last Pieta. But you did not covet them, you held them in your heart's affections, you continue to see them in the mind's eye — so look all you can, be happy. What are you afraid of now? Do not covet or cling. Remember that wonderful black writer who said in her poem,

here is what I have —
poems
big thighs
lil tits
and
So Much Love."

Later that evening the delegates had all gathered arriving from Japan and Korea and Malaysia and Manila and Australia and New Zealand. They were at the poolside near a wall covered in orchids. They stood drinking gin and tonic and guava juice and wine and nibbling sea-food canapes. And the talk turned to ageing and death because many of the delegates had last met four years ago under different skies and were now exchanging health notes and ageing parents. They ate and drank and grew pensive under the stars and yet they all felt far from all that; "all that" of course being ageing and death, far from all that. That is why, she thought, we can all talk of it at all and so bravely and knowledgeably. Pretend we know it all, know about old age and infirmity and the "thousand natural shocks flesh is heir to." Dear Henry James with his, "live all you can, it's a shame not to." Perhaps that's why we have rushed around all morning buying things because we plan to live forever, to be slim again, and more than trim again and wear little black strappy dresses like all the will-o'-the-wisps we see here. After all we are only sixty-one years old or just sixty-two.

Her mother was only sixty-two when she died. My father must have taught her, his wife, to look and admire and not covet. Her mother had travelled to Karachi and Lahore and Delhi and Hamburg and Paris, Zurich and

London. In her mother's cupboard they had found after her death a small gold mesh evening bag and in it a small piece of jade, a handkerchief embroidered with roses and a small bottle of Chanel No.5. Dry sediment of perfume, but everything still most fragrant. Had he let her buy these things or had he given them to her? Of course he had. Gifts are important. Gifts have meaning over and above. Things also last. Her mother had kept them. That night she dreamed again. She dreamed a most terrible dream. A dream of going home to her parents' home; everything was chaos and great movement of people who were not her parents. She did not know who they were. All the doors were wide open and there were packing cases strewn all over the lawn and tea chests in the driveway. Strangers carrying things out of the house and putting them into the chests and there was a hammering sound of nails being driven into wood. And she went frantically from room to room looking for her parents, calling out to them, "But where are you, where?" At last she found her father quiet and unperturbed in his study. But there were six men in his study with machines and piles of books everywhere. She picked up one book and then another, then another and they were all her father's Everyman series of Shakespeare and Chaucer and the Victorians and Socrates and Thucidides and Burke and Ruskin, faded green and rusty covers with their deathless inscription, "Every man, I will go with thee, and be thy guide. In thy most need, to go by thy side."

And she asked, "But what is happening, what are they doing, these are your books, why are they piled everywhere?"

And her father said, "They are taking them back, they

are going to where they came from, where they really belong."

"But they are yours, they are your books, yours, your name in them, and the date in each of them in your own handwriting, they are not borrowed. They are part of your precious library."

"No" her father said, "They were only lent to me for my lifetime. Now they must go back, these men have come for them."

"But they are yours," she said desperately, "Your most valued possessions."

"Do not distress yourself, they were lent to me and their time with me is up. I read them and reread them, and yes, they were my most important possessions but they must go where they belong now."

"But what are these men doing with their machines? How do they dare? Why? They will harm them, you must stop them. Why are you allowing this to happen?"

"They are recording for me my favourite passages. When I was a very young man and then a not-so-young man I used to mark and underline certain passages. Do you not remember when you read them you noticed the marking, the ink turned brown and sepia by then? Now I will never have to be lonely for them because these men are recording the passages for me, for always. The books will go but their essence will be with me. No need to grieve. It was an agreement made at the very start. And now the men have come. I myself was ill prepared, had almost forgotten that they would come, my time has come, I did not know, but they knew. So it must be."

"But you said, you always said, 'buy books, books last'."

"But that's just it, they do, they have. They last you lifelong. Your whole life is the books you have read and how you have read and learned from them, how you learned joy and sorrow and how to face everything and almost anything that comes to you in your life to face. And of course they last. It does not now signify, it does not matter that they are taking away this Everyman series. I have them in my mind, in my life, in your life. The trains crossing rivers and dusty plains while I read and read, the river and stream and meadow, park benches I sat in in Felixstowe, the grass of Delhi, by my window at Oxford, in a tent in Sind. I do not have to possess or cling to their physical beauty to smell the precious paper and binding, feel their covers in my fingers. How else do you think I could have borne the loss of your mother for twenty-two-years — I have her essence. Of course there is a part of one that grieves, that longs, that misses, we are only human. But no clinging. I will miss this Sophocles, this Aeschylus, how it felt to read these men and what they left behind for us — the time I was sixteen or twenty-one or seventy-one. What things I learned, what revelations they contained for me, the excitement. But that's nostalgia, nothing to be gained from nostalgia. It's the worst evil, only to long for some particular moment, to return, to relive, its smell, its texture, the whole business of wanting to have it back. You cannot have it back. It's gone. You have to move on. Time goes by." As the dream began to fade she asked her father, "I know you don't believe in it but what would you want placed on your *Khatlo*, that last ritual? What? Because you are going, aren't you? This is what you are trying to say to me?"

And he smiled ever so gently, ever so sweetly and said,

"Come, let us walk in your mother's courtyard near her *champak*. If you must play out the ritual then I'd like to be certain of your mother being there, so one of her white cotton saris, and chappals for her feet and my spectacles, and many books. You know some of my favourite ones. Oh yes, I grow greedy, my transistor radio for the BBC six o'clock news."

She woke up with such an intense desire to be with him but his voice was gone, he was gone, and something kept repeating "pictures of the mind recall that table and the talk of youth."

On their last night on their way up to bed they passed a large poster of a beautiful girl. "Chantal Astin sings for you tonite and every nite — at the Kaspia Bar," and the hotel bulletin read in gold letters I.F.A.A conference Rm 8, Fiona Wong's bridal Shower Rm 9.

On an impulse they stopped and went to the Kaspia Bar and Chantal sang the song they asked her to; "you must remember this, a kiss is just a kiss, a sigh is just a sigh, the fundamental things apply, as time goes by."

Next day at the airport she made her way to W.H. Smith and asked if they had the new Booker Prize winner, *The Ghost Road*. And as a voice called over the speaker, "Passengers for Singapore Airlines Flight 338, this is your last and final call. Please proceed to gate no. 53," they found her book, she paid for it and rushed forward to gate 53 thinking, Yes, oh yes books last.

14 A Green Flag for Shana

It happened one day quite suddenly, as they say; something snapped. Shana decided she'd had it. She'd had enough — thanks very much. She went to the door of her room and said that's it — I am never leaving my room again. If anyone's listening, I am never coming out of my room again. Ever. It's final. Her husband had said to her, "How could you have so little pride in yourself? You really are fat now — really fat and if you don't do anything drastic it's really over for you." That's when it happened. That was the final trigger. This from her husband hurt her the most and there was nothing more she could do. She really had tried very hard. And this was the unkindest cut of all. She would not put up with it any more, no more chattering voices, no more snide remarks, no more rudeness. And that was that. And it really was.

Her bedroom became her sanctuary. You knocked before you went in. And you went in only if Shana acknowledged your knock. The bedroom had shelves filled with books. Shelves filled with magazines and newspapers. And cupboards filled with food, not clothes. Shana did not need her clothes any more. She shovelled them out of her cupboards and threw them out of the room that fateful morning. She kept some nightwear and a few large caftans and all the rest she threw out of the room and locked her door. The servants were frightened but there had been fights before. It would all turn out all right in the end. They shopped for biscuits and chocolates and cheese and everything Shana asked for and they stocked the cupboards. In the centre of the room there was Shana's bed and Shana lived in that room. She never left it except when she was carried out.

In the years and years in the bedroom she saw her son grow up and get married. She saw her husband die. She saw her granddaughter grow up. She felt deeply the death of her husband and she adored her granddaughter but she never left that room. The room had one comfortable chair that was for her to sit in while her bed was being made and also for any guest she might have. All her meals were in that room and all the in-between-meals were in that room. Her visitors, one at a time, to talk with, to listen to, were her contact with the outside world, and of course her books and her newspapers. She had a flowering bougainvillea in her balcony and the branches came into the room. She never went out on to her balcony. There was too much life outside to look at and young slim girls rushing in their jeans and skirts and tights and T-shirts. She was not going to look at all that. For the last five years Shana had been putting on weight. A great deal. She had also tried to do a great deal about it — she had gone to doctors. She had gone to slimming workshops. She had eaten soya nuts and bran *atta* and *bhusa* bread and bottles and bottles of homeopathic pills. She had not lost one pound. She went to a health farm where she starved and took mud baths and drank carrot juice and nearly died of the horror of the routine but though she cried from hunger she never lost weight. At a party the evening before her drastic decision she heard a remark made by a man she had known five years ago. As she came into the room she heard him say, "But that can't be Shana, I know her so well — that's not her". Shana had blanched and then hardened herself and walked up to him and said, "Of course it's me — have I changed so much? You have changed but I recognize you." She decided to stop trying and the next morning her husband had said that.

A life cannot be lived like that always thinking about what people thought, or what people said about the way one looked. Of course, I've lost the fight and I'll never be slim again and hate this new self. I really do hate it. My God when l think of the months and months of green leafy vegetables and hateful soya nuts and soya biscuits with young slim gazelles all around leaping about, so careless of thin beautiful bodies. Little do they know — she had thought — it happens to the best of us. And she did not wish them well in her heart of hearts. She had started to wear huge tent-like caftans and watched her jaw-line disappear and her cheek bones disappear and knew she was doomed. She daren't look in the mirror any more and she knew she was fat, was fat, was fat.

Now in her room she felt safe. I shall not be looked at by other people — only I will know what I look like and what I feel. I will not be laughed at and pitied by other people. This is my new life. And I will stick to it no matter what, and she did. She never left her room. After her bath each morning she went back to bed and stayed there. She read her books, she ordered books. She read the news-papers. She knew who had died, she knew what concerts were on and what plays were being performed. She knew who was getting married and who had had a child, who was divorced and outside the rain would come down for months and months and then turn to heat and more heat. January would become February and the year would pass — and then the years would pass. Did pass. She never left her room.

And so as the months and years passed, Shana was quite at peace with herself, sometimes when people rang her up, she said, "Come over and see me, lots to talk about." Sometimes she was cold and acerbic, "Yes, yes I know who's calling. Is there anything in particular you wanted to talk about because I'm extremely busy."

But most people forgot that they could see her and speak to her. She became a kind of legend. People would point to her flat and specially her bedroom counting the years she had lived in there. The bougainvillea spread and spread and its branches left blossoms on her floor and sometimes on her bed. But then she fell very ill. She'd had a good innings, a very good innings all things considered. All that eating and no exercise at all. And early one morning she died.

Many people came to the house and sat or stood awkwardly in their grief at something they had never really understood. Then they went one by one to her room to pay their last respects and came out crying or just shocked and speechless. The room was so still and quiet. The body in the bed so still and quiet. The shelves with so many books and the flowering bougainvillea dropping a blossom or two. And then the stretcher bearers and the hearse and the long quiet ride to the cemetery. At the cemetery the scent of new and old flowers and wreaths and the sounds of pickaxes and earth. And then the placing of the body in the grave. She had wanted to be in the same grave as her husband. Shana would have been pleased that there was no problem, they fit beautifully in the single grave. The granddaughter like a young gazelle planted a young bougainvillea on the grave. And when we looked up suddenly at a terrace overlooking the cemetery, two women waved a green flag for Shana's stubborn life and for her safe passage.

15 *Set My Heart In Aspic*

Gino of the "Esperance".

Well, I don't know how exactly it started for the others. I mean how can one know? Ever? Or even if one knows, only in bits and pieces, never the whole. So anyway this is how it began for me. I remember exactly.

I had finished all my chores on the yacht and I was feeling like land. Nobody had called for it, there were no orders. I needed a rest from taking strangers for a spin in her. Most of them just wanted a bit of smooching or more, away from prying eyes and hardly looked at the sea or at the clouds and the wind in her sails. The yacht needed a rest. She needed a quiet by-herself sort of day. And I, as I said earlier, was feeling like land — was feeling restless. I know what feeling restless can mean; I needed to be off again on a long journey. Really long. So it was best I just hooked off and did something different. Maybe just for a day, maybe two.

Borrowed a motorcycle from one of the beach hotel staff and took off. Goa often reminds me of home. That is if I think of home as being Sicily. I suppose that is home. It's where I started. More ways than one. Of course if you asked me in what way Goa was like Sicily, I wouldn't know. But then you're not asking me, are you? Anyway, it's something, I don't know whether I

could begin to explain. It's something. Not just the
obvious — like sea. Sea and sky and sand and rock.
Because it isn't that. All the colours are different. The
textures are different. I'm comfortable here. I'm not
comfortable in England or Australia. I liked the sailing,
mind you, but not the long time I had to dock — to
re-haul or replenish whatever. But Goa, yes. Here I've
been docked for over two months. That's long for me.
And I'm here not uneasy as in a strange place. I don't
feel a stranger here. I feel I've been here before. There's
some connection. Some long-ago memory of this place
as if at some deep area of myself. I was bound to
something. I don't know what. I'm not given to thinking
too much. Or if I think I don't really have to work on
it. Who would I do it for. I don't have anyone to analyse
things for? I have thoughts. That's it. I have instincts
about people, and places and the sea, but then I let go.
Why should I hang on to it then? Later reference? To
tell someone? To have someone listen? To write to
someone, and have them write back? I don't have any
of that in my life. Long ago — yes. But not now. Not
for a very long time. Not to worry. I don't. Anyway I
reached this village and stopped. Felt like a cold beer or
just a need to stop. And that's when it started. As I started
to drink this beer under a tree I heard a church bell. You
don't hear them much, though there seems to be a church
or chapel at every turn in Goa you don't really hear that
many church bells. So I heard it. In the quiet — or out
of the quiet after the noise of the bike as I drank the
beer I heard the bell. Solemn, rather deep, a not-often-
tolled sort of sound and coming from quite near. I was
hot. I thought of cool interiors of churches. I thought

of my mother. I walked towards where I knew the church would be. It was very hot by now and I longed to reach the cool — at least the imagined cool of churches in the villages of Sicily — and in a small clearing I reached it. A small village and a huge church. At least the façade was immense, massive white-washed rising out of the red earth. And in a corner of the clearing a spreading *gulmohur* tree and massed bougainvillea of every colour and a very small group of people. A priest. I watched them for a while and perhaps should have realized that it was an occasion of some private solemnity, but I walked into the church; for the cool and the sense of my mother. It was dark and huge and cool and empty, and the smell was as in a Sicilian church a mixture of candle wax and old flowers and old people. I sat down and I waited. The priest came in and walked to the altar. The bell stopped. And four women in black walked in and went to the front of the church and knelt down. Later I realized it was five — I didn't realize I was counting. And the service began. I was an eavesdropper, but no one had asked me to leave or told me I should not be there. Perhaps because it was a church after all. It was not a family chapel. Anyway I was there. And I became a part of what I saw then and after. What I didn't mention was that there was a coffin with flowers. Also, ten minutes after the service began another woman came hurriedly into the church carrying something which she gave to the priest and he blessed it and placed it on the coffin. It was an urn. The woman sat next to the other women. She looked different from the others, somehow. Her hair was loose. I mention this because most young women either have short hair or hair put up in a bun or at least braided. This woman's was long, was free and open. I realized she was a woman. No longer a girl.

After the priest had spoken about the dead woman in the coffin he spoke of her daughter, and I guessed her ashes were in the urn, then he blessed each of those women who came up to him and then placed flowers on the coffin and on the urn. After a short silence one of the women stepped to a kind of carved podium and sang a short song and said it was for her mother, and her sister. She had an extraordinary voice, trained but natural and very moving. She sang in English and the words were from the song of Ruth — "Entreat me not to leave thee, or to return from following after thee; for whither thou goest, I will go; and where thou lodgest, I will lodge; thy people shall be my people, and thy God my God. Where thou diest, will I die, and there will I be buried; the Lord do so to me, and more also, if ought but death part thee and me." This is what she sang.

Then another of the women went to the podium and read from a scrap of paper. Of course by now I realized they were an unusual family here in Goa, in this setting; it was like a play, the enactment of something universal. I could not move, I did not want to. Could not have even if somebody had asked me to leave. This was a family. I had become part of it. These were the words she read from her scrap of paper.

"Be not wanting in comforting them that weep, and walk with them that mourn. Be not slow to visit the sick; for by these things thou shalt be confirmed in love." Then the woman with the long hair unbound came and said these words with no paper in her hand, "My mother recited this often, I think she longed to attain this. She had a difficult life and I think we made her life very difficult to bear. We cannot now undo that but I remember these words of strength. The master said, 'At fifteen, I bent my heart upon learning. At thirty, I had planted my feet upon the ground. At forty, I no longer suffered from perplexities. At fifty, I knew what were the biddings of Heaven. At sixty, I heard them with a docile ear. At seventy, I could follow the dictates of my own heart; for what I desired no longer overstepped the boundaries of right'." Then she said, "Since our sister Mathilda could not say her words for our mother, I will read the last words that she wrote for my mother in her journal. This is what she wrote. She had changed the gender. 'Vex not her ghost; O! Let her pass; She hates him, that would upon the rack of this tough world stretch her out longer.' "

There was a great silence after this. A terrible quiet as though the sadness was not to be borne. And then suddenly we were all outside in the bright hot sun, again with the flaming tree, the great dazzling façade of the church behind us, looming over us and one of the women came towards me and asked me to join them at their home for the wake. I did not hesitate. I went as if I had known a long time ago that I was a part of them, that it was inevitable. It was as natural as the leaves that come to a tree. The small group moved towards the house. I had forgotten all about the motorbike. I was a part of this here and now. We went in and somebody closed the door.

I could not see for a moment or two. It was almost as dark and cool as when I had entered the church. And then it was all right. I saw the long hair, a hand outstretched with a glass in it, a long-stemmed glass with a pattern of vine leaves on it half filled with a greenish gold liquid, " 'welcome to our home', Mama would have said," and she turned to speak to the priest.

At this point there is really something I have to speak about and that is I'm not any more a young man, nor even a youngish man. I am forty plus and then a bit. For me it's not a problem. You're young and after a bit you're not so young and at the work I do there's no problem, later of course — I hope much later managing a pretty large yacht on my own may become a problem. But who's thinking that far? What I really wanted to say was something had happened to me in that church, and now it was even clearer to me — about the woman, the one with her hair open to her waist, I felt something stir. Truly. Some part of me asleep a· long time, stirred. It seems absurd. But it was real, that is why I mention it. I wandered about the large room with blinds made of shells and old carved furniture, portraits on the walls, a rocking chair with some embroidery on a frame. An unfinished rose in a cluster of fern. The ferns were completed. Only the rose remained. On one table there were photographs in silver frames. I bent to examine them. In one family group there were the parents and four girls sitting and kneeling beside them. In another just the four girls. One, my girl and three others. In another the woman who had sung Ruth's song with a man and two little girls. After a while I thought I should go. I looked around for someone to thank, someone to say goodbye to. One of the sisters came to me and asked where I lived. I said that mostly I lived on my yacht. And she said, "So you have no address."

I said "No except where we are docked."

And she said, "We?"

And I said, "I and my yacht."

She said, "Oh. So how will we find you?" This was the girl with the long hair. And I said, "You must come to my yacht. Would you fancy going out to sea for a short trip? We are docked in Dona Paula and most of the time I am there. Most days I take people from the hotel for picnics. I would be honoured to take your family." She was watching my face and then asked where my home was, and I said, "The yacht."

She persisted, "No, your beginnings, where you started from, where your mother lived."

And I said, "Sicily."

She said, "That's a faraway place. Mama would definitely have said, that's a faraway place."

"Well, it is definitely further away than Dona Paula. I am so glad I came to Arpora. I could so easily have gone to Saligaon. They say, the guide book says, there is an unusual parish church there, different from all the others. But I liked your church very much. And the tree outside."

"Yes it is beautiful, only it hasn't its own cemetery. We are buried in Nagao. Close by. But I wish it was here. Mama and Mathilda would feel closer. I suppose that's silly considering that for the last fifteen years we have all been living with oceans in between."

"But tell me again how did you come to our village and to the church today? I mean of all days."

"I came on a borrowed bike, which I hope, for the sake of its kind owner, is still where I left it. I had been riding for a long time and then I got hot and thirsty so I stopped for a beer, and I heard a church bell toll. And that's how

I came to your church for your family funeral. I was fortunate. And fated."

"You have come very far from your yacht, but I'm glad that you were fated to stop in our village. Did you know that our small village is very famous?"

"I didn't know but I must say it ought to be famous for the beauty of its daughters."

"No, seriously you must come again and visit us and I will show you our village. Will you come again, soon? Say yes."

"Yes. I'm so glad we met and that I was part of that beautiful memorial service. I shall never forget it. I must go now and I will see you again on my yacht — It's your turn now to come to my home. I hope you will not disappear as suddenly as you appeared in the church."

"Yes, that was terrible, terrible. The urn with my sister's ashes arrived very late. Anyway I hope they will be peaceful now, in their own village. Come back to rest from such a very faraway place."

She put a small hand in mine, and kissed the air first one side of my cheek and then the other in the Goan way and I longed for this moment not to end. It did. I said goodbye to the others and last to the priest, and left. When I looked back they were all standing on the porch and staring after me. I raised my hand. I hoped.

Therese's account

I'm the sister who is married, and teaches music. Piano. That is how I am described, in Arpora. I'm watching my sister Alcina talking to the strange man who was in the church. He doesn't seem strange to her. I asked him where he lived, he said on his yacht. If Alcina has anything to do with things, which she always does, we'll all be marched off to visit him on his yacht. Alcina has no pet name. She wouldn't allow it. Even when she was very young. She is very firm-willed. My name is Therese. I have no nickname. In the early days before my daughters were born my husband called me Theresena. He must have some term of endearment for his mistress. I have no hesitation in mentioning this. It's not unfair he is not here. It's simply a fact of life. I sound quite tough. I'm not. But I am the eldest. Mama taught us that we should always put up a brave front. When I asked her "why — or for who?" she said, "for yourself, for self-worth, for carrying on, for dealing with the humiliation." And so on. She knew of course. What did she not know? She seems to have known even before we got married. In that same blessed church we were in this morning. Of course everyone knew. Arpora is famous. But then it is also famous for being very small. We do not live here — for that I must be grateful. There is so little to be grateful for in this, our life. Mama would have said immediately 'Nonsense'. We live in Ribander. There is a road that seems to cut through a house and a church. We live in that house. I am constantly reminded of church and so-called higher thoughts, and then instantly reminded of this noisy actual world because of this road, that, as I said, cuts through. My life, my music. Well, everything. I used always to have a great many students. It's different now. Even the older, better families now have a dreadful instrument called a Yamaha. Some used to say shame-facedly, "We had to get rid of our grand — the last time the piano tuner asked for air fare from Dalhousie!" So it goes. My life.

Anyway here was my sister talking to a strange man in the family drawing-room, our mother dead, our sister dead and she was behaving as though it was a party. I suppose it was in a way, that was what a wake was supposed to be, a fine sendoff for a dear one. Mama would have enjoyed it very much. "Drink up, there's more where that came from." Our sister would have enjoyed it somewhat less. Alcina had arranged all this. And she had done it long-distance. The priest, the church, the flowers, the ashes, the memorial and what they would do and say and read and sing. Everything. And she didn't even live here. Hadn't for a good fifteen years. And she made it all seem so natural. Effortless. She looked wonderful too. I look middle-aged. Boring. Look at my shoes. I don't know what she thinks she is wearing but she looks beautiful. And her hair. Mama would never have allowed the rest of us to wear it like that. "Simple", she would have said, "it suits her, and look at her hair." It was true. If I sound as if I dislike Alcina, I don't. I envy her. That is all. I always have. It's a habit. Even long-distance. Of course they all blame me for not having been here for Mama. When she needed me. She never needed me. Not ever. They thought Mama loved all of us equally. This was just not true. No parents can. They try to hide their preferences. That's all. Anyway, I was the only one who did not desert Mama. Also, living close by doesn't always make anyone feel closer. Or wanted. I have my pride too. Anyway, I didn't go waltzing off to faraway places when the going got rough. Not like Sweetie and Alcina. They were jealous because they couldn't have Rui. Rui married me. They just couldn't stand that. Why else do they all dislike Rui? He's someone they all wanted.

And couldn't have. As for Mama they probably poisoned Mama's mind. Made her hardhearted about him. He was so handsome. Nothing like Rui had ever been seen in our gloomy old house. They should have cut most of the trees down and put in a lawn. But no, they had to have dark trees with the hope of orchids. "Pride, think of the untruthful life you are living under the same roof as that scoundrel ... leave him and we'll work something out." It was easy for Mama to write that. All that old fashioned stuff. Honour and, "daughter of this house" and stuff like that. It was unbelievable. In this day and age. I liked my home away from gloomy old Arpora and its brooding ways. Here I could hear the traffic and see the sea and the river and far away Piedade. I liked playing my piano, I liked teaching piano, and I was singing again. I pretended I did not care about Rui because I could not see my life without him. He was always nice to me. He always came back to me. He lived here. He was my husband. I'm told it happens all the time. In the best families. How else do you account for the amazing green and grey eyes you see? Anyway. He lived with me and I was his wife. I pitied Sweetie and Alcina going to faraway, lonely, places and I was certain they would never find husbands what with their odd ways.

Mama always liked me the least. And I always minded. She was always comparing me with the others as if she admired them more. And because of Rui she despised me. I know. But I love Rui and I always will. So though I have chosen a safe life, closing my eyes to many things, I'm settled. Till this happened to Mama. And it's true. I never came to see her except for that once. I could not bear to see Mama in that bed not moving, not able to speak, just looking at me or rather something beyond me with her beautiful, white hair spread out round her thin face. Just looking at me but searching for someone else behind me, perhaps Sweetie or Alcina, not me. Not me at all. And they were not here. I never went back. Who wants to visit someone when the truly beloved faces are not there. After all I too have my pride. My own kind of pride.

Mathilda's journal

Well, this winter it was a real shocker by any standards and all the heating devices frozen, and icy winds and rain to make it all much worse. Outside, it was brown and grey and the tree outside my only window with black branches, was slippery wet. And then one night the snow came dropping slow and soft and we woke to a fairy-tale morning, everything bathed in white and it still kept dropping feathery soft. It felt warm like magic. At night it gleamed silver. It was a delight to the heart and I took Mimi for short sharp strictly 'pee-walks'. But then it went on and on and hardened and it was difficult to remove the snow piles and there was a fearful screeching of car tyres and brakes all the times. The snow was two feet high and then four and then people stopped trying to clear it away and even the snow machines could not do anything to help. It began to look and feel like some ghost city. I watched it from my window. It shut out everything. And then one day into this frozen unreal world Faustina's letter came in the post. About finding Mama in the garden with her sunhat and her secateurs on the ground. She had had a stroke and Tessa was nowhere to be found. Poor Faustina. I do hope Mama leaves the house to Faustina in her will. She deserves it. Not one of us does. We all deserted the house. We all deserted the house and Mama. Faustina stayed and tried to manage. The letter was dated weeks ago. It must have been the wretched weather that had caused the delay. I tried ringing Goa but all the lines were down, frozen I'm sure. And so I sent telegrams to her and Alcina and Tessa. I felt so alone. I kept thinking of Mama lying in her walled garden with the old well with its red-black stones and steps, its guava trees and the huge old mango and the three coconuts. It was that day, the day of Faustina's black news that I stopped injecting myself with insulin. At first it was because I wasn't thinking of anything normal or routine. I only hope I fed poor Mimi. I stopped caring. I didn't even take my emergency pills. I tried to walk Mimi on the slippery sidewalks and then suddenly Mimi collapsed. I managed to half carry and half drag Mimi upstairs. But she couldn't eat or drink anything and I couldn't get hold of the vet. Mimi died. On the third day Mimi died in my lap. My close, beloved and dearest friend died looking at me with her beautiful golden head and her deep-sea eyes. I buried her with the enormous help of the janitor. It took half a day of digging, the ground was frozen so hard. I buried Mimi's red collar and leash and her two feeding bowls. It's fairly simple when it's a dog. Even if it is a friend of fifteen years. I hear her all the time. Her nails tapping on the floor, I keep hearing her coming into the room or following me. I keep turning round. The sound she made when she settled down the whole length of her on the floor, following me settling down next to the chair I sat in, following me to the bedroom, the bathroom, the kitchen. I cried and cried for Mimi, and for Mama to get well, to speak again, for me to be able to say sorry for having moved to such a very faraway place and never going back.

I have always been the coward among us. Alcina the brave one, Tessa the safe one, and Mathilda the coward. Afraid of the dark, of low-flying fruit bats, of sudden noises, of separation, of death. And that's why I came to this faraway place in the first place. To prove to myself that I could and I should be on my own. And after Rui married Tessa, I could not bear my life in Arpora. Dear familiar Arpora, but small gossipy Arpora where everybody knows of everything, where everyone knew or guessed how I felt about Rui and it was Mama who said, "Yes, go to your faraway place, I'll miss you very much but he's a bad one that Rui and Tessa will rue the day she married him and I'm sorry he had to be your first way of finding out about loving someone. First love is the worst in terms of suffering but strangely it does stop one day and you wonder how you could have agonized so desperately over someone. Here in Arpora you cannot forget him. Tessa will manage in her safe way. She'll pretend, she'll sing, she'll bear his children, she'll forgive him long before she forgives you for loving him. She'll humble herself. She's not the first. She's not a bad girl. She's not unique. She will play the piano and she will try not to think of her life." That's what Mama told me and even when I was packing. "But come back to this house Sweetie as soon as you can bear to. I shall be waiting." I tried always to remember that. I could have gone back when I was over him. I could have gone back to Mama from this faraway place. I could have taught in the old school. Anything. Mimi would have loved the garden and the large cool rooms. Arpora and its old houses and the church, the sea so close, the saltpans and fields even closer, the old grey house with a tower. I really let Mama down. She helped me to go away. But I didn't help her by going back. When I could. I've really not changed. Deep in my body I've not forgotten Rui. Never, not in my deepest heart's core. He came here once and of course I saw him. How could I not? I've never grown leather as they say so colourfully. I'm down to the wire. What a vivid term to describe *in extremis* states! Better than anything the French could think of. Or the Portuguese.

Mama, I really miss you. Perhaps I never should have come to this faraway place. I never made friends. I only met and truly loved Mimi. The only real person in my life. I missed Alcina and I wish we could have lived in the same city. I've nothing really to show for having lived away from home for fifteen years, and that's a long time in a life. Away from home. Fifteen years. Away from Mama, fifteen years, and I'm fifteen years older. Grey in my hair quite a lot. And Mama must be quite white. As I think of Mama, I think of her so, this is for her,

Vex not her ghost;
O! let her pass; she hates him,
  that would upon the rack of this tough world
  stretch her out longer.

Alcina, her account

Alcina holidaying in Mexico got this letter on her return.

"Sweetie died last night in her apartment. You are not to worry about anything because all things considered, her doctor said she died very peacefully in a coma. She had stopped taking her insulin. The place where she worked said she had taken two weeks' leave as Mimi was ill. There had been nearly ten days of the most difficult snowfall and it was difficult for her to commute anyway. So nobody had seen her except the janitor of her apartment who had helped her to bury Mimi a few days ago. She had a very bad cold. She was found by the janitor who went to her apartment because her milk bottles were collecting on the steps. You could not be traced so we had her cremated and her ashes are in an urn that you could take back to Goa for your mother. I think you should go to Arpora so that you are together with your mother as she will want to bury the urn in Arpora. Your mother need not think of it as suicide but because of the diabetes which your mother knew about. I think she committed suicide. She had a supply of insulin in her apartment. It must have been the loneliness and the silence of the endless snow. And of course Mimi who she had loved for fifteen years. Try not to think about that too much. Because it becomes too impossible. To bear. And none of us with her.

"It will be a sad reunion but I am sure you agree it would be important for Mama and for us. And for Sweetie. We had a simple ceremony at the funeral parlour. We chose some of her favourite music to be played. We even unearthed *Jesu Joy of Man's Desiring* and a fine version of *Sheep May Safely Graze*. I hope Sweetie heard, wherever she was. Is. I'm glad her dog died before she did. Not for Sweetie but for Mimi's sake. At least it's one less person to grieve. I do not know how we are going to break the news to your mother. We cannot write to her. We must be with her. She only has Faustina with her. And you can't trust Tessa. She must still be mooning about her life with Rui. Rather without Rui. At least Papa doesn't have to grieve about this. There's something to be said for being dead."

As Alcina read this letter she thought, "The nickname Sweetie was so real, it suited her so well. She was so dear, so really sweet, so dear to all of us. We were lucky. And now bereft. Mimi had been so lucky being found just a few days old under a car, huddling in a cruel world. That had also been a winter. Sweetie's first in New York. We had spent a lot of time together those first few months after Sweetie arrived in America, alone and sick at heart. Still in love with that bastard Rui. We had gone together looking for a place together, the best bargains — cold garages and even colder basements. Old lamps and rugs and her own bits and pieces. And one day we had discovered Mimi. Very small, very golden and Mimi and Sweetie had adored each other from those first moments together, fifteen years ago. Where had time gone? We had both been in our twenties and Mimi a few days old. Sweetie had photographed Mimi often and she had grown to be a big golden dog with wonderful eyes and coat like a golden Retriever and husky, all mixed together. Big but very gentle. Very possessive of Sweetie. They would have killed for each other. Died for each other. Oh Sweetie, I wish I had been with you and not on that stupid holiday in Mexico. We could have talked this thing through. Life will never be the same without you. How will we bear this? How will Mama bear this? What words will we have to tell her? How will it be done? A brother would have been so useful. Tessa was impossible, she's probably still jealous of Sweetie, perhaps Faustina? It will be me in the end. I know.

Dear Sweetie and loving Sweetie why did you have to

be alone? And the snow and the cold. None of us were with you, not one. What was she thinking, what was she suffering and feeling? Did she try and contact us? Snow outside, huge funeral mounds of snow. The colour of death. And this was to have been the year, almost the month, for going back to Arpora, to Mama, to the house. Mangoes and fish curry and rice and sarpotel and sitting on the balcony in the evening and Mama doing her eternal needlepoint roses. So many cushion covers, so many chairs. Why did Sweetie do it? Can things ever get that dark, that black? Loneliness. And no point anyway. It was not to be borne.

Faustina's account

And she was always watching the door. I know it was because she wanted to see your faces again.

Of course now all of you have come and I'm glad she was spared having to know about Mathilda. I wonder though whether she might have known. Somehow I hope not. Now that it's too late all of you have come. Mind you, I am only telling you all this because Alcina asked. It relieves my heart to be able to speak of it. It was too much to bear all on my own. I'm grateful for your having asked me to tell you. And soon I may be able to cry — to cry and grieve for Dona Gabriela properly.

What can any of you know about what it felt like looking after Dona all those months since her stroke? You saw her lying so peaceful in the church. What do you know? How can you guess? Can you imagine what it was like for her? And for me? Day after day filled with awful slow moving hours and terror-filled nights — those were the worst, because she hardly slept, never seemed to close her eyes. With a small night light left on for her, for me, and the Queen of the Night bush from her own enclosed garden sending in such an intense fragrance. How green her fingers were! She was planting something even the day she had her stroke. That's where we found her, in the garden with her sunhat on and her secateurs lying near her. She would lie all night and just stare and stare at this awful thing that had happened to her; if only it had taken away her mind, her feelings! She would just lie and stare as if she could not have enough of the sights left to her. Often I thought of bringing in your father's portrait but then I thought it would be like he was calling to her to join him when she was not yet ready to go.

And the worst thing of all was her not being able to speak. That was the worst. Not being able to eat, not being able to speak — that was the very worst cross she had to bear. She would press my fingers, she could look a certain way, she could make certain sounds which we had learned to recognize and knew more or less what she wanted. But only basic things. Never any of her heart's desires. The sound when she wanted to be turned on her side, or when she wanted to be relieved, or when her head ached unbearably. For her agonized heart we could do nothing. I used to try hard to know her thoughts. And she never gave up trying. The therapist came twice a day, and she tried to do the exercises for her legs and arms, her hands, her feet. One terrible night, as though she had not borne agony enough, her shoulder slipped out of its socket and she howled like an animal. Her weak muscles would not hold her arm. She grew so weak we could trace each bone, each nerve almost. And her food. What food? The doctor said the minimum requirement was 1100 milligrams a day. If we managed that it was a day to celebrate, but mostly it was barely that, then half that and then it was just impossible, it caused her to need suction even after two spoons of juice. It was pathetic. I could not bear so-called meal times. That is every two hours or so. I dreaded it because she might not take anything. And if she did, how triumphantly I measured it and wrote it down and underlined it in red! What food? While she had the Ryal's tube we could give her all sorts of things to nourish her. She even had an excellent, very creative dietician, but she developed ulcers because the tube was in so long, three months, so then it was teaspoons. I still cannot bear to look at a teaspoon. Orange juice with glucose and honey, sweet lime juice, electrol, coconut water, apple juice, mashed papaya, mashed banana, clear chicken soup, the greatest day was when she had half an egg! It was pathetic. I would keep going to the bathroom to have little weeps. I daren't cry in front of her. What she would have said was "Faustina in ill thoughts again? Men must abide their going hence even as their coming hither." How much she had taught me! And now she could not speak. And in four months and three days we did not let her get one single sore on her small body. Not one. That is in nearly one hundred and twenty-four days as she got thinner and thinner she did not develop a single sore. We had been told such frightening stories of patients even in the large hospitals with sores so large you could put a fist inside. Where the patients had died from the agony of large sores turned septic, died not from illnesses but from sores. We even worked on bags filled with glycerine to place between her twisted legs. And she did not get a single sore. Not one. And when we washed her hair it was shiny and white and lay around her face and pillow like a young girl's. Her skin became so soft and pale from just lying there day after day. We used bottles and bottles of eau de cologne and talcum powder and she smelt so sweet. And her nightgowns, we made her wear them back to front, with fastenings at the back so nothing ever troubled her getting it off her from over her head or neck. Oh, we did everything to make her comfortable. But we could not make her speak — ever again — we would never hear her voice ever again. I longed to hear it. Even her voice shouting at me in anger or irritation. But that was never to be.

Alcina

And one day when the funeral was long over and the wake and they were all, even Rui sitting in the balcony, Alcina said I shall not be going away again. I have thought about this quite a lot. I shall stay here. So Rui you can forget your plans for tying things up with this real estate shark and your five-star ideas. Casa Cunha is mine now as it is. I shall ask Faustina if she would like to stay with me as she always stayed with Mama and always looked after Mama. I shall be making some changes of course — because I need to feel that there is running water all through the year. Also fans in all the rooms and Gino can stay here while I'm making these changes. He's very good with his hands and I find him very necessary. I shall mend the gazebo in the front garden and train bridal creeper over it, very pink, I hope. Also in the back garden instead of just wild bushes we could have some wild almond trees so that the leaves could turn red and orange. I shall want to look out at things and Mama always took trouble about the garden. I shall repair all the broken tiles everywhere and try and get old beautiful ones to match. The roof needs looking at and all the cracks that have appeared. All the blinds have to be redone and our great wrought iron gate that now leans dangerously sideways needs to be propped up and the pink bougainvillea that trailed over it seems to have died. The front garden will look wonderful with the betelnut trees and the two old *champak* trees. I shall not cut the tall wild pampas grass because I notice the weaver bird or its descendants still like it for their nest. I can't think why I ever went away. There was always such goodness here. Oh yes, also the house and the compound wall ever so whitewashed. It's going to look marvellous, this house, and I'm going to live here always. I hope Mama knows this. Also Sweetie, I wish we were all together again. Perhaps we are.

Also I must tell you that Gino is very important to me. Very. So this is his home as well. His yacht will sometimes be my home. So I have two homes. So I shall not be so restless. I'm young yet, and Gino makes me feel younger than I have ever felt. Mama and Sweetie will not see this as a betrayal, that I now enjoy the sun on my skin and the taste of mangoes and smell the intense sweetness of the Queen of the Night again. Of course there is the sudden lurch of sadness that they really have gone forever, but that must pass, in time. I have lots of that. Mama would have loved us all back again, all sitting on her balcony at peace. Except of course Rui — but even he is welcome as long as his thoughts are kind ones. The oddest people have been known to become nice. So why not Rui? Life has a way of going on. It really has a way of doing that. And in the strangest way, don't you think?

Doesn't anyone want to say anything? Day following day, eating and drinking, dung and death and life. Oh yes before I forget I have to get rid of the crows. I don't remember there being so many, they are driving away all the other birds that used to come. I shall get a gun. I saw an advertisement a few days ago in *O Heralde* for a gun and I shall write off to the address. It was sandwiched between the obituaries and the Thank you to St Jude, it said "Loud bang for picnics or stage. Send only Rs. One hundred. Rs. ten extra for postage," somewhere in Jaipur, the address said. The drawing of the gun was funny and frightening enough for any crows that dare to come to Casa Cunha. And I think that's all. Except I have come home to stay.

16 *Wintersmoke*

As of now,
we all know what to expect, but their generation
is the first to fade like this, not at home but assigned
to a numbered frequent ward, stowed out of conscience
as unpopular luggage.
As I ride the subway
to spend half-an-hour with one, I revisage
who she was in the pomp and sumpture of her hey-day,
when week-end visits were a presumptive joy,
not a good work. Am I cold to wish for a speedy
painless dormition, pray, as I know she prays,
that God or Nature will abrupt her earthly function.

— W.H. Auden

I am not argue-proof   — W. Shakespeare

To get to anywhere you really start from the lake; the
lake really dominates the place. If you get lost you just
try and get back to the lake and start again. The lake
is large but not too large. You can walk around it quite
easily. Cycling round it takes about fifteen minutes. It
used to take me fifteen, now I take half an hour. But
that's cycling at an easy pace so that you can look
around and be aware of things. Because it is a beautiful
place, almost all the year round. As you cycle you

become aware of trees and flowers and old garden walls and the sound of the lake at all times. Little pathways smelling of pine or eucalyptus lead off and up from the lake, and you take one of them. There are butterflies and bees and the odd blue kingfisher taking a low dive into the lake waters. I go to Wintersmoke everyday except Sunday. I work at Wintersmoke. I don't get paid though it is my job. I work for an agreement that one day when it's my time or turn I will be allowed a cottage at Wintersmoke and I will be looked after.

Wintersmoke is an old people's home. One day I will be an old person. Here I will have my freedom, but also I will be looked after. I will be protected and I will feel secure. You must wonder what my job is and as we still have a little way to go I shall tell you. I read to the inmates. I also write their letters for them and read their letters to them. I help them with their gardens and their pets. It is a long day and often on the way home there is the sound of an owl, and fireflies cross my sight. The lake is dappled with light. But most evenings I cycle home at sunset with everything rosy and still warm. My home is a rather bleak cottage. I live alone. The children hardly visit and I can hardly remember the sound of my husband's voice. Mum made me marry a seafaring man and that's how I lost him, I think. Oh, there was a time when every shore leave was a miracle of love and excitement; of course I was pregnant every year till I learnt about the pill. There were longer and longer gaps. And then less letters. And then my letters started coming back. And then I never saw my husband again. The children grew up and went away. I had the cottage and I made jams and marmalade and sold it to the hotels and I baked bread and tarts but gradually my fruit trees stopped giving me the wonderful fruit of so many years. I suppose it was a case of atrophied vagina, me and the fruit trees. But strangely they did still blossom every year, so that was a miracle to look forward to. Also of course the sudden blue, intense and true of the kingfisher, and the low-flying swallow. The loneliness got better gradually. I did not share my pain or my life with the inmates of Wintersmoke. That would not have done at all. That I would save for later when I lived in my cottage up at Wintersmoke. I knew my turn would come. I am plump of figure with nice eyes and thick curly hair. My husband loved my eyes and hair, now I am still a little plump even with all the cycling I do but my hair has a lot of white in it now. Curly still, though. The children adored their father, naturally; which child could resist a father who came back once a year? Presents and a lot of spoiling, no disciplining. A party every day. All the wretched stuff left for Mum. He had his uses of course. Mended the ladder so that he could mend the roof. Collected wood, made the fires every evening. Made love as if he cared. Oh yes, he had his uses while he lasted. Much later I heard he had another family, in another country. But as my Mum said, "You can't expect too much in this life — or what would there be left to look forward to in the next. Look on the bright side."

The inmates of Wintersmoke had much sadder lives, so I try very hard to remember my Mum's words. "Look on the bright side." And that is how it really began. I started writing letters and I lived in those letters I wrote

every week, everyday for the last ten years. As I turn
in at the tall white gates I am met sometimes by Mrs.
Maitland. She is very tall and very thin — my idea of
how Mary Poppins might have looked. She is the most
bitter of all the people who live here. She always says,
"I want him to come here just once — only once so that
I can spit on him. That is all. Just once. It's not much
to ask for, and no revenge really for all that he has done
to me. I wouldn't say a word to him. Just look at him
and then spit. He'd know why, and it would please me.
I think of it a lot. I do hope I don't die before he comes.
I think it's what keeps me going. The thought that he
must come, small and slim and impeccably dressed. A
real dandy if you must know, sandy-coloured hair thin-
ning even then, small moustache, it used to tickle when
he kissed me, I used to have to stoop down for him to
kiss me. We both worked at a radio station. He read
the news. I did book reviews and a classical music
programme. That's where we met. New Delhi during the
'40s. We never had any children. I collected books. He
collected carpets. I had a wonderful collection but his
was spectacular. Prayer mats from Kabul, and carpets
from everywhere, beautiful carpets of the most won-
drous weaves and subtle colours. We never missed
having children; we worked and we collected carpets
and books. Now I am just a ragged old woman with
white straw hair urging a toothless old dog, one step,
another step and then another to the old bench from
where I can see the lake. One day he'll come puffing
up the lane to Wintersmoke to visit me. That's when I
will take him back to my cottage and let him look at
the carpets — and when the old look comes back into

his eyes at seeing their glory, I'll spit on him. I hate him.
I really hate him with a cold icy hate. I wonder where
his little Burmese woman is. I know they had six
children. I have three times six carpets. I'm sure he'd
like to trade his six for the carpets. I'm better off than
he is. Even though I keep pain killers and biscuits in my
oven. I believe it is the doom of men that they forget.
I can never forget. Like the Jews. They can't forget."

Mrs. Maitland told me her story in bits and sad
pieces. I felt I had known Mr. Maitland. Talking of
Mrs. Maitland and Jews urged never to forget, brings
me to Cottage No.2, Dorote. Hamburg 1939. There
lived a professor of German literature at the university.
He lived in a wonderful house and gracious garden
with his wife and twin daughters. He loved Rilke above
all poets though he read and thought most widely.
When the book burnings began the twins were sent to
safety on the last boat to Australia. In a diary to be
read when the twins were twenty-one they read of how
one night their father the professor poisoned his wife
and then himself. Of course it was written as the last
entry in the diary. The diary had a few addresses of
friends. One was an Indian family who **had** lived next
door to them in Hamburg. A family of husband, wife
and four daughters. The last baby had been born a
fragile two pounds in weight and had lived in an
incubator for two months and had a dear German
nurse called Elsa who looked after everybody. The
diary gave their home address in New Delhi and it was
underlined in green. There was a note in their mother's
hand which urged the twins to contact them in trouble.
"They are very kind, they will always help, they shared

much with us. Turn to them when you need help and love, your Mutti." This diary was in Cottage No.2. Often I read bits of it to Dorote. Specially the poetry copied out by the professor. The Duino elegies seemed to be what he was reading at the end. Dorote loved them the best and one Christmas we had found a precious old copy in the old library and somehow kept renewing it — it was still in Cottage No.2. It was loved as the Bible. When Dorote had first arrived at the place on the lake she had come with her twin sister, Elie. They loved each other dearly, walked together, read together and planted together a quite beautiful garden. But Elie was always fragile in health and died one spring morning. She is buried in the cemetery near the lake under the trees. Now Dorote wants to join her sister and cares less for the garden and I read a lot of Rilke to her. She thinks too much of all the deaths in her family and the reason for them. She and Elie had spent a lot of time planning to go to Israel but they were too old for the journey. Her favourite elegy she repeats often, goes like this:

O trees of life, what are your signs of winter?
We're not at one. We've no instinctive knowledge
like migratory birds. Outstrip and late,
we force ourselves on winds and find no welcome
from ponds where we alight. We comprehend
flowering and fading simultaneously.
And somewhere lions still
roam, all unaware,
while yet their splendour lasts, of any
weakness.

I found Rilke very difficult at first but gradually I

listened to him very carefully while I was reading and began to understand him. Now I find him very necessary, everyday. A garden teaches this. "We comprehend flowering and fading simultaneously."

And so I come to Cottage No.3. Here lives or partly lives Sister Stella. I can hardly bring myself to talk of her. But she is safe here, though she cannot believe she is safe any more, here or anywhere else. And she cannot sleep and hardly eats and is torn apart by guilt and fear.

Sister Stella was a nun in a small convent in these hills. Quite a remote place. I went to fetch her from there two years ago. A small beautiful chapel, five nuns and a few whitewashed cottages. Being nursing sisters they did much to help poor villagers in the hills around. Sister Stella drove the old Landrover. She was a good mechanic and a good sister of mercy and medicine. One late evening while the sisters were at prayer, a gang of men broke in and frustrated at finding so little they could steal, raped and killed four of the five nuns. Sister Stella badly hurt and in shock crawled to a hiding place and we brought her to Wintersmoke. For two years she didn't speak at all. Now she hides under her bed at dusk, and shrinks every time she sees a man, even kindly Dr. Fernande walking down the pathways with his wife. She asks me over and over why God had not looked after his people. She did not pray. She cannot pray. She wished she had died with her sister nuns. Cottage No.3 is the one I dread the most. There is nothing much I can do in the way of comforting. I feel like saying something she often says, "Comforter, where is thy comforting." She has nothing in her cottage to remind her of her former life. No cross, no Bible, no holy pictures. She wears a skirt and thick shoes and has allowed her hair to grow out. She is pretty, she came out from Ireland, she is forty-five years old. She helps in the vegetable garden, is ruthless with turnips and weeds. She digs frantically often pulling out quite lovely wild flowers.

Sometimes when it's time to go into Cottage No.4, I stop in the garden and look, sometimes at the lotus pond at a dragonfly drunk with sun and freedom. The scent of the garden at Wintersmoke is wonderful. I wish some-body could bottle its scent for a wine. It's not a garden in the formal sense because it becomes woods and has an orchard. In spring it's like a Japanese garden or fan made of pale pink paper blossoms. A sudden storm can bend many of the old trees and batter the *raat-ki-rani* creeper. And after a rain shower the tall stately cannas look like bedraggled large dogs' ears and legs flapping and wet. And when winter comes all our trees look like Christmas trees without the toys. Oh yes, here the seasons really matter, really change, autumn the saddest because it heralds the end and is so royal, so gold, so scarlet. Seasons do we comprehend flowering and fading? The lake has all the answers. Our quiet lake hardly shifting, moving, except when a boat glides past or a lonely fisherman catches something silver and it thrashes for one brief moment. Of course sometimes the lake is glassy and pale, sometimes glass turned dark and fearful but mostly peaceful with mists rising out of it, or a fish. It's the sort of lake where you feel if the Arthurian legends had happened here then this would have been the lake from which — "an arm rose up from out the bosom of the lake, clothed in white samite, mystic, wonderful."

Cottage No.4 has, in its little porch, climbing rope and pickaxe and a lantern. These things are never moved they wait in readiness. A retired tea planter lives here. We all dearly love him. Bob we call him. His tea plantation was in the blue hills. He lived there all his life. His wife and daughter were great trekkers. One summer they trekked to the Himalayas. A crevasse, unseasonal weather, rain and then a heavy snowfall for a cruel month. Their bodies were never found. Bob went to look for them with rescue teams over and over till nobody would go with him any more. When Bob was finally brought back he had turned into an old man. He refused to live in his tea plantation so he was brought to us. He is a great favourite. Snow-white hair, the bluest of eyes. He could be eighty, he could be seventy-five. Actually he is just sixty. He listens to a lot of Telemann and Scarlatti and reads and waits for his family to come through the door. He never leaves the grounds of Wintersmoke just in case they arrive when he is not here. He blames himself terribly for not having gone with his family that summer. For not making the time. "I could have helped them, I could have helped by just being there." His cottage looks out on to the lake. He never looks at hills or mountains. He is afraid. He waits. Sometimes I listen to music with him. Sometimes he shows me his album. Photographs of his plantation, of the family, of his home, the dogs. Actually I know what everybody's family looks like except Sister Stella's of course. Dorote has a family album and so does Mrs. Maitland and Dr. Fernande has one too. I feel a part of all they have been part of. I know what they all looked like, the people they long to see again, the homes they once lived in, I feel I know it all. Also of course I write their letters for them and wait for replies that never come. Often I write pretending replies. I go to the old club library for them with lists of books to borrow for them. Their lives are really more real than my own. I have very little time for my own life. It suits me.

Dr. Fernande and his wife live in Cottage No.5. They are not well physically, also they are heartsick. Alzheimer's and athritis. But they do not complain and Major Parkins, our medical man at Wintersmoke, calls on them everyday while he is taking a constitutional. They are waiting for their daughter Nina to come and be with them before they die.

She is never going to come but they are going to keep waiting. I know. I wish I didn't. But I do. Over two years ago there was a letter from her which God forgive me I opened and then tore up. It said, "Don't write to me. Don't try to contact me any more. I don't read your letters any more. I have a life of my own. There is no place in it for you. I have never needed you and have always hated the life you gave me, and I hate the lives you live. I have changed my name. I do not read your letters. I do not even collect them ...." I tore that letter up and now write letters from Nina to her parents. I hate Nina but I have made her into at least a decent daughter, if colourless. Here is a sample, I have it here in my pocket. "Dear Mama and Papa, It was wonderful to get your last letter. I long to see you and I soon will. It is difficult because the child is so young. India is so far away. I miss you very much and wish I had never left you. I am so glad you are at Wintersmoke, I envy you. I feel quite jealous of Suzie, she seems like a daughter." (Ho, hum.) I just make up as I go along. I have begun to hope that Nina will never come. She is a monster of selfishness. But then again their need is very great. And they have waited a long, long time. They are patient but they are not going to live forever or even for a very long time. Waiting for her is killing them softly and surely. In their cottage is a prized possession. A small mahogany carved desk with ivory inlay work on each drawer. In each drawer are very neat and tidy drawings and crayon houses and flowers and happy families done by Nina when she was a child. Also Nina's school reports and sports certificates and medical cards and photographs of her as a baby born to already elderly parents, and photographs of her each birthday in a new birthday dress, then as an adolescent and so on and on. I hated that desk. Every visit I had to get the key from its careful hiding place and open each drawer and share the contents with them. They are very gentle people and talk to each other in Portuguese.

Monday is clean linen and laundry day. Tuesday is letter getting and reading day. Wednesday is cottage dusting and heavy cleaning day. Thursday is Major Parkins' medical inspection day. Friday is baking day. Saturday is getting ready for Sunday. And Sunday is going to church for some or just resting. No gardening on Sundays. The music from Bob's cottage on Sundays is religious music.

And so our lives are filled with each week. Soon I shall have to get up from the bench with trees above me, the ground under my feet and far below, the eternal lake. I have come to the end. These are the cottages and these are the present inmates who live in these cottages that make up Wintersmoke. My name is Suzie, Suzie with a zed, Mum always said. And I will end my account with a bit of my favourite poem from Dorote's father's diary. It is this;

There remains, perhaps,
Some tree on a slope, to be looked at day after day.
There remains for us yesterday's walk and
    the pampered loyalty.
Of a habit that liked us and stayed and
        never gave notice —

17   *La Loire Noire*

Valsa was to accompany her husband to the Loire Valley
— to a conference as a wife, not as a delegate. But she
was really going because of a postcard she had got from
Varun at Christmas and that was six months ago. Not
the usual long letter and cheerful card. Just a postcard
of a river with poplars. Loire River. France it said,
explaining.

On the plane to Paris she couldn't get to sleep and
arrived disoriented. She felt strangely dislocated for the
whole precious day they had before they caught the train
to Tour. A Viking exhibition being much publicized, they
went there. They spent the whole morning there and in
retrospect she realized the fear had begun there.

It was a striking and frighteningly mounted world of
Vikings. Creatively set on two floors with steep steps
leading up and down and the area was crowded with boats
and horns and fierce headgear, battlegear, weapons, all of
dark wood, dark, hard leather and iron, gleaming horns
and spiky things. Nothing blonde and blue-eyed about
these Vikings. Everything here was fierce and violent,
huge black and white photographs of black waters and
rocks and waves and sky. Valsa thought there is blood and
more blood, dried black blood and bones. A Viking poem
declared quite sparely.

Cattle die
Friends die
Thou thyself shalt die
I know a thing
That never dies
Judgement over the dead

Next afternoon they left by a very fast train for the valley. One of the delegates played solitaire on her lap never once looking up and out at the changing landscape. Her husband drank and swore nearly all the way about a lost suitcase, about the "frigging" train, the "frigging" French and their language. After one rather louder outburst the solitaire wife looked up and Valsa saw that she looked like a clean, clear, ugly, elegant, aloof Ali Mcgraw. She played on quietly. A man with blonde hair and very blue eyes handed around pieces of goat cheese and wine from his vineyards, he said he was of pure Viking stock. And though he smiled and handed around goat cheese and wine she thought "cattle die/Friends die/Thou thyself shalt die —"

As the sun began to sink the train stopped. They had arrived. The road to the chateau where they were to live followed the river all the way and it was lined with poplars and they were not Hopkins poplars, 'hacked and hewn', but tall and supple with the last rays of the sun shining through them. Valsa looked and looked for an old wooden bridge with an old houseboat tethered to it, "Let me not be too late, dear God," she prayed. As they arrived it began to rain and it was cold, but friendly voices said, "Not to worry, a little unseasonal weather, tomorrow the sun will come out and it will be warm." A lovely young boy took them up to their room, up and up a steep staircase, almost to the turrets, a beautiful room with a sloping roof and large window looking down on a pool, a tennis court and the poplars, an avenue of poplars. Though birds wheeled about in the sky Valsa could hear only the low hoot of an owl. It was not night yet but an owl looked at her and slowly closed an eye. Like a wink. The owl had winked at her. "Cattle die/Friends die" — "Rubbish, I am not superstitious and certainly not regarding a friendly neighbourhood brown owl." From the tennis court shouts of encouragement and then abuse came up to the window. It was Ali's husband, "Mind the ball," he yelled, "or it will land in the sodding pool" — Valsa lay down and closed her eyes forcing herself to think of fairy tale castles of Walt Disney or the Grimms brothers or Hans Anderson but, all she could see in her mind's eye were fierce Vikings and the clang of chains and hard, dried blood on leather. All night long the owl hooted and she could not sleep.

Next morning she woke to the sun shining through the poplars and then rain began — a strange light Valsa had seen long years ago. The road to Pahalgam, sun and rain through poplar leaves. Forty years ago, silvery green unearthly light and a white horse riderless pounding down the avenue. It seemed to be more unicorn, mythical beast than horse. It was another lifetime. Another life. Was it hers? All morning and afternoon the wives were taken to see famous castles with tapestry and rich awnings and banners of silk and fleur de lys and great Renaissance landscaped gardens and great four-poster beds but Valsa felt great fear because there were always the dark, dark echoing dungeons and tunnels and stone cells and winding staircases and great drawbridges and huge cauldrons for the burning pitch to upturn on enemies and moats with dead fish and green scum floating and clinging to slimy walls.

Though it was May Day and little children sold bunches of fragrant lily-of-the-valley, Valsa thought of hot tar and impaled heads and the terrible dark waters slapping against stone and great wheels turning on cobble-stones.

That night she screamed and screamed and her husband woke her and comforted her saying, "It was only a dream, a bad dream, everything's all right, wake up, wake up." Valsa fought her way up through cobwebs of dreams. In her dream they had been looking for the tennis ball and then they dragged the pool and a white-green body floated up and up through the green scum. Gold-red fish darted through the fingers of the body and the mouth and the sockets of the eyes and it was Ali. Valsa called out, "She's dead, she's been taken out of the pool and there are gold-red fish and there's a tennis ball at the bottom of the pool." They went to the pool still in their night clothes and the air very cold and they stood there while the pool was dragged. All they found was a tennis racquet and a tennis ball covered in slime.

By then it was morning. So they drank their coffee hoping that the sun would shine bright and warm and that the evil thoughts would not return but the voice persisted, "Cattle die, friends die, thou thyself shalt die —"

Valsa wanted to see Ali and her high-swearing husband run around the tennis court calling out, "Mind the frigging ball or else it will land in that sodding pool." Two white pigeons dipped low over the pool and then flew up and away through the poplars. The air was very chilly.

Cold really. Somewhere there must be rain. She must find the old houseboat tethered to a very old wooden bridge. If only the sun would really shine warm and life-giving! "Where's that bloody ball got to then?" All that old heavy tapestry and awning, what lay behind it? What did it hide, what had it seen? What heard? She asked the young boy who had brought their luggage up on the first day the name of their chateau and he said smirking, Le Parc aux Cerfs — the deer park. And Valsa asked if there were still deer and he said, "No, no deer, it has a double meaning, it means young girls — the king would come, hunting for young girls, not deer." She saw handsome, large King Henry VIII type kings hunting down young tender girls, chasing and hunting them in these great carefully land-scaped gardens, chasing through tall, perfect mazes and herb gardens. Poor young girls panting and running and unable to run any more and falling. Yet in these parts they said there was such a love of poplar trees that every time a girl child was born a poplar tree was planted. A girl was a gift, she had thought. Now she knew. A girl was a gift. Free gift to a handsome, large, tennis-playing king. With an older wife and mistress doing careful minute needle-point. Things are never what they seem to be. Life is cruel, cover it up with tapestry and heavy awning, suck and lick the bones clean and throw them on to the rush covered floor, young chickens and young girls. Sharp, pointed teeth rip and tear and flay the skin. Skin from bone. And that evening dinner was arranged in one of the caves of white clay this valley was famous for. Again a fairy tale on the outside but inside the cave dripping cold walls, cave ceilings dripping cold water drop by drop on great dark hunks of meat so rare the blood still flowed.

Great goblets of wine red shining in the candlelight and Valsa realized she'd got through all these days drinking wine. The wine had warmed her, the wine had kept her slightly off balance, not of this world but out of this world. Valsa told herself you are just pissed out of your mind, that's all, thank God for the wine of this valley. A young counter tenor sang a new old song and the group grew quiet listening in the dank cave of white clay — things simply lasting, then failing.

> to last — water, a blue heron's
> eye and the light passing between
> them into light passing between
> them into light — all things
> must fall, glad at last to have fallen.

Tomorrow I must do what I came for. Tomorrow I must follow the instruction on the postcard. Please let the sun shine. Just for tomorrow. I could not bear to meet the faces I must meet, in the cold rain. Valsa said these words as she lay down to sleep.

The next day, being given free for two whole hours, Valsa walked to the road that ran by the river and she walked and walked. Finally she came to an old houseboat. Her postcard had said visit us if you can but soon. Jason is hanging on but only just. He's nearly gone. We are in a very old houseboat tied to the oldest wooden bridge. Hardly any traffic where we are. Come, but soon. I need a little sanity in this hell of pain Jason is going through. All love, Varun. And now she had found the old wooden bridge. Valsa hesitated and then climbed the steps and climbed aboard and knocked at a wooden door. Almost immediately Varun came out and hugged her hard and seemed to be crying. She hugged him back saying "Don't cry, don't cry" — and Varun said "I'm sorry this is a luxury I do not allow myself, but I've been so alone and now you are here. It's miserable day after day keeping cheerful for Jason, sometimes I feel I will die of it — are you ready to see him?" They went into the small bedroom and there was Jason, dear Golden Jason propped up by the window staring out. Valsa watched him for a while not daring to go any closer till she was ready. Jason was paper-thin and his face and his arms were covered in what looked like burn marks, long lesions sore with ooze, no hair on his head, but when Valsa stepped forward his eyes shone and seemed to smile. Valsa smiled back and held him carefully as close as she dared. She sat on his bed and Varun went into the kitchen to open the bottle of wine she had brought with her and to put the wild flowers into some water. Jason said, "I'm so glad you have come dear girl you must take Varun back with you or at least make him promise to go. It's too much for him and now he must leave me. You must do this, he will never do it on his own." Varun came back with three glasses and they toasted "friendship" and spoke of old times and also of Varun's mother and the messages that she had of her longing to see Varun and when was he going back to Bombay — his mother missed him so much and Jason of course. She didn't get about much, she said I was to make you both promise to go back even if for a short holiday. Varun said "she doesn't know about Jason. I couldn't tell her —"

"Yes, I understand but your mother senses that something is very wrong, because you never went back home for Christmas or the New Year or Easter and you usually do. What about your job, have you paid leave or what? Tell me." "Yes, I have leave and I try to write my music as regularly as I can …. They have been very good to me."

"What is your new work about?" she asked and immediately regretted being so stupid but Varun said, "it's about this old boat and this river and the water sounds and the breeze through the poplar, sounds and sunlight and moonlight and Jason — really it's about Jason."

"It sounds very ambitious, is it nearly finished?"

"Yes, it is, and no, no it's not nearly finished." Jason had merely sipped his wine to toast their friendship and was really not with them any more. Varun said he did this all the time now, all through the day, he sleeps but it's not really sleep, it's to help him bear the pain, the body just seems to switch off and he's so weak. I have some medication for him but mostly at this stage it's tranquillizers and pain killers — otherwise he'd never make it for even an hour. It's terrible. It's worse than any word can describe. You know he pretends he can see, but he is practically blind now…." Varun had his head in his hands.

Valsa said, "Will you come back with me?"

"No," he said, "I'll not leave Jason. He has not got long and for his sake I'm grateful for that, but he still clings. I hope he doesn't cling too long. It's terrible to watch him and see the change in him each day. You read of it and see films about it but till you are really in it you can never know — never be really prepared for all the humiliating things that happen. It's hell and it's worse then hell. I feel guilty at being able to hear music and to write music but also I know at its deepest level it's the only thing that keeps me going and of course I'm grateful that Jason sleeps almost all the time — I feel the agony is bearable then for him. But you dear friend who came, what of you? What of you? We two go back so long a time — how are you? And how did you manage to come?" Valsa explained about the conference and Varun said, "A miracle, in short and how long can you be with us?" And Valsa said tomorrow it ends, tomorrow we go back and just then Jason opened his eyes and smiled. He said, "You know I sometimes dream I'm as I was, that I'm well again. No pain, no sores, no humiliations, small or great. Varun and I eating and drinking and working and walking together." After a while he dropped off again and slept. Valsa and Varun went on deck and she asked, "Are you all right?" And Varun said "Yes and no, I have some symptoms but I'm still all right — for a while. But I'm done for, I shall go the way of Jason and I'll not have Jason to keep me going. He and I have no child to leave behind for all our five years together that's why I want to finish this piece of music before it's too late, I want it to show everything we've ever meant to each other all these years. It's all our lives together. I wish we could have gone together but I suppose it's never like that for anyone. Jason does not know I'm sick, it's the only untruth that lies between us. He'll have urged you to take me back with you — he has, hasn't he? But you know why I cannot. I cannot take this back with me to further sadden my mother's life. I regret nothing so much as leaving her so many years ago, never marrying, never giving her grandchildren — all that. I have a lot to answer for but I can never regret my years with Jason. I have been greatly blessed. It could so easily not have happened. Do you remember the music I wrote for that adaptation of the Book of Job and St Thomas' Cathedral and the great north window? I think of it often and I truly believe that this was the illness God cursed Job with. This was what Job suffered. Jason has suffered nearly every stage of Job's agony. Job was a good man, Jason is a good man. Promise me that when I send you the finished music you will try and see that it's given a chance to be heard. I need three great voices and a cello, a flute and a harpsichord. Promise." "I promise," Valsa said and kissed and hugged Varun and left the houseboat. "Promise to visit my mother," Varun called after her and Valsa called back, "Promise".

"Bless you and safe journey" he called and she said, "and you likewise". She hurried. Now the poplars had begun to look gloomy with no sun shining through the leaves. She hurried, frightened and lonely till she saw the lights of the chateau shining through the darkness. I'll never see Jason again, and I'll never see Varun again. Cattle die/Friends die-'

The next day they left the Loire valley. They had a day in Paris. Walking after dinner they came to Saint Germaine du Pres propped up by scaffolding but inside a musical offering. Bach and Pachelbel. Sitting in candlelight with eighteen other people Valsa listened and thought this is a requiem for Jason and for Varun. I shall never forget this solemnity, the scaffoldings, the music and the shadows that the candles throw on the walls and the great ceiling. The organist knows the pain of people and the aloneness of people like Jason and Varun alone on that houseboat. He is playing for them and about them and watching over them, passing down their river like a dark swan.

Next day facing an airport and then the journey home. Valsa was ill for a very long time and when she slept or when she was awake she saw not her home or the food they ate or the books in the book shelves or the paintings on the walls, she never heard the familiar voices on the telephone. She saw only dark swans and white pigeons and a brown owl. She saw tall poplars in rain, she saw a wooden bridge and moats and drawbridges and dark towers and dungeons and girls in white dresses running and running through forests and heard a hunting horn. She was quite lost.

But one day after many months the post brought a parcel of sheet music. It was dedicated to, "my friend Valsa and to my mother." It was called 'La Loire Noire.'

18 *Rites of Passage*

The father's story

I could of course be considered very fortunate — it's a matter of perspective really. As when someone rather old dies, some persons say to those who are grieving, well, he had a long life, it was time for him to depart. But there are ways of perceiving the truth of what old can be in different old persons. There is the old man in his eighties not good for anything any more, physically and mentally, a burden to himself, longing to shake off these earthly shackles. And then there are the others also in their eighties full of a fine agility, a finely tuned life, a love of fine books, of food, of flowers, of music, of family love, of much work still to be finished and even begun. What of them? What does it mean to console by saying, "he had after all a long life?" And how long is this long life anyway? Most of it is so taken up in babyhood, extreme childhood, in long years of learning, then in waiting to put some use to what has been learned. Then all the mistakes made or the wrong or even right turnings made, then the peaceful times. Hopefully. The taking-stock time. The all-passion-spent times. When do these come? Three score and ten. Long and fruitful life. It's a laugh. I digress. This business of perspective is what I was thinking about. I could as I said earlier be considered fortunate at having participated so closely in the several rites of passage of my daughter. I was there for nearly all the semiprecious ones and all the most important ones. Her being born, her marriage...

It is not given to all parents. There would of course be another way of looking at this. I really do see that. But since this is one way to look at and feel about this — I have chosen it. The other way — well, even this stout Englishman might remember a long-ago heath on which a father howled, "never, never, never, never."

The first rite was the birth of my daughter. Many years later it pleased my daughter very much to know that she had been born at home, with a midwife to assist my wife. Not a hospital. It was too far away. My daughter thought it was a conscious decision on our parts. It was not. Our village is miles away from a hospital. But our church and the graveyard very close. The second rite was my daughter's baptism. This took place in our village church. We gave her an old name. Part of this landscape. Part of this family. From all this you will have gathered that we were an unexceptional rather ordinary family. A conventional couple from a small village in England. Lived there all our lives — till of course those two unusual journeys. But our daughter was rather different. Children are different from their parents. We never credit that somehow. I suppose, to think of them being in the same mould makes us feel safe as houses. Rather the known than the — and so on. But our daughter, even for these odd times when young people are being or rather are doing unusual things, broke the mould completely. Not just the edges. With her even the basics were odd — take eating for instance. I don't think you can get more basic than that. She never seemed to eat food, I mean food as we understood it. Even when she was a slip of a thing she held out quite firmly, even when disciplined. We never struck her or punished her or anything, but she just dug in her heels — and that was that. Her school seemed all right, so we never knew where her ways came from. Certainly not from her friends. They all seemed from their size and shape generally to manage on what most people ate or drank. Not our daughter. She could never be tempted by her mother's wonderful fruit tarts or jellies or even chocy mould. Not even the Wall's ice cream lot. With her it seemed to be just various forms of vegetables, grass and herbs. No milk, no cheese. Naturally she had nothing to do with flesh or fowl or even the fresh catch I came home with at the weekend. Anyway she grew. And alas, away. She read avidly but never at any stage her mother's childhood books, no Enid Blyton or Angela Brazil or none of the Katy books or *Little Women*. She did read an old copy of that book about cruelty towards otters and later she read a lot of that other writer whose titles were so beautiful, *Ring of Bright Water* and Gerald Durrell, so we felt that maybe she would become a vet and a new kind that used only old herbal medicines. As she did not believe in western medicines she would not touch anything we used even for headaches or toothaches. Oh yes, I forgot to mention she found old books on herbs and flowers and plants and travelling to the places where you could collect these wild remedies. And so she grew and her mother died when she had just turned sixteen.

She went on to college and it was wonderful for me when she came home every vacation, short or long, to be with me and ramble the countryside. I suppose I should not have been too surprised when she took a doctorate in Eastern Philosophy and Indian languages specializing in Sanskrit and Bengali. I would say she's well on the journey to becoming a monk or a female version of a swami as it is called. And then came the difficult time for me and her when she decided to go to complete her journey, to India. She wrote to me very regularly and I loved it when her long letters started coming. I would read and reread them gazing out from time to time at the rusty autumnal coloured Japonica bush my wife had planted just before our daughter was born. In one letter she had joined an ashram outside Madras and then some months, several months later, was teaching yoga and forms of meditation in Bombay. One day a letter where she spoke a great deal about a man she was teaching in her class. Later another letter asking me to come to her wedding. Of course I went packing very carefully some old lace that belonged to her grandmother, that I felt she might like to wear on her wedding day as her mother had done before her. There was no question of my not going though it was the longest journey I was ever to make; how could I not be with her on the most important day of her life?

It was a long flight and I knew I might have to go to the ceremonies straight from the airport, so I had on my best dark suit and was nervous and wished my wife could have been with me. Her, that is my daughter had told me, young man's mother was a widow, had been widowed rather recently, also she had just lost a beloved dog called Golden Days. It sounded like the Japonica bush. Golden Days. She must be an interesting woman to have thought of such a name. I had a long time to think a lot of thoughts. I wondered what my son-in-law would be like. My daughter had said he composed and played music. He read a great deal. He did not fish. He did not play cricket. He was very kind and gentle, he looked after his mother.

Well, the wedding ceremonies were unusual. To say the least. It was also very beautiful. There were a large type of orange Indian marigold everywhere on the ground and hanging in long garlands like rope and my daughter put one in the lapel of my suit. My daughter did not wear the old cream lace because she was wearing a red cotton sari. Her feet were quite bare but for a deep red intricate painting of flowers and leaves. She looked very pale and thin but very happy. She had flowers in her hair and I wished her mother could have seen her.

And so another great rite of passage had been crossed and I left for home lonely leaving my daughter with her new husband in her new home in another country. Her mother-in-law was a sweet distracted woman who seemed very fond of her son and new daughter. I knew my daughter would be cherished. I felt left out and sad. Suppose most fathers feel this when their daughters get married, but I felt like the only father in the whole wide world who had ever faced such lonely emptiness as I did on that long flight home.

A few weeks later there was a long distance call from my son-in-law. I had never heard his voice on the phone before and thought for several moments that they were here in England and asked if my daughter was here as well. It never crossed my mind that anything was wrong. He said my daughter had cerebral malaria, she was very ill. She refused all the medicines she should have been taking. He sounded close to tears. He was in tears. I was too when I told him there was no medicine she would take. I left within the hour for India. And this was to be the very last rite of passage I would be part of. The very last one, the final one of all, the rite that no parent should have to participate in. Of course she was too weak. And it was all so useless. And she died of course. What else had I come for? What else had I made that long journey for? My daughter died. She really was all of a piece. You have to give her credit for that. Her hatred of hospitals, her belief in wild flowers and herbs and plants. She died for all that, and her fierce beliefs. And I wept and bemoaned the fact that I had not an ordinary girl who liked Wall's ice cream and her mother's chocy mould. I wept for all those wasted years and her youth and her stubbornness.

And so my story or rather her story ends. There is no other rite. This was the mysterious unfair final one.

Home is very sad now. There is no one here any more. Except me. Of course. And the Japonica bush that will live longer than my daughter.

The mother's story

I think we have always been an odd family. If I said an unusual family it would probably be another way of looking at it. But then I am not trying to offend anyone — they are my family. I too am part of it, though I must say most of what happened to it seemed to happen in spite of me. I was there for most of it. I was married a very long time ago though I am still quite young. I have a grown up son and a daughter.

My husband before he died Read. I am saying that as another wife might say my husband before he died was a lawyer or a doctor or a teacher. My husband Read. From the time he woke up in the morning, having read off and on through the night, read, went to work, came back and after his cup of tea and a bath, started to read again. Many wives I have watched, rush to bring their husbands their chappals, for tired feet, or gossip a bit about what happened that day or tell him what was for supper. But not this wife. From the day I was married to him till the day he died — I had only to bring him the book he was currently reading and his spare reading glasses. He was a very quiet and good man. His eyes were bad. He hardly noticed me. With him there was no point in my changing the way I dressed, or wore my hair. I was not part of any book he was reading. Or had read.

In this way life carried on. On the way our three children also grew up. We cannot really understand how or when this process was happening. I think all parents feel this shock but they cover up very quickly by pretending that they had watched every step of the way. When they read a great deal it was easy to say, yes, they have taken after their father. But when our daughter began to sing very well and grew very tall I, for one, could not decide how this had happened and when. It seemed that only yesterday I used to oil her long hair and plait it for her — sometimes putting a red ribbon at the end of it. But suddenly without telling anyone she broke free, got herself a scholarship and went to the States. The following year she sent us a photograph in good colours. The photograph depicted two tall strangers. One was a very tall girl with very short hair and the other was an even taller American man. At the back it said simply, "we are married", and the date. It was about this period of time that my husband died. One Saturday evening he was reading as usual and I slipped out to get some coffee at our nearby stores, and when I came back he was still reading. I made his coffee and brought it to him but he had slipped a little sideways, his book on his lap and the bookmark on the floor. That is how I found him. He was very quiet, I could hear the clock ticking. He was quite dead. For him it was peaceful. But for myself I would have liked to have said some words to him. Or heard him say something to me. Of course I realize that in these matters we cannot choose. After sometime my son came back from his yoga class. He was not alone. And that is how I met the English girl. It was late evening, a Saturday, my husband was dead, and here was a new person. For a few strange moments before I could say anything, I thought my son had brought a doctor. That somehow he knew and had come home with this person who would make everything well again. Or at least as it was before. Long ago when I was a child I was very ill and my father brought a strange doctor to our home. He was not like us. He was tall and white and spoke English and placed a cool white hand on my forehead. This person that my son had brought home with him was also tall and white. Not like us. She was not a doctor. She was my son's yoga teacher. She wore a sari, she had chappals on her feet, her long hair was twisted into a bun. She was an English woman. She did not go away. She stayed and helped us at this sad time. With my daughter far away I really would not have been able to manage everything that has to be done when a person dies, there are so many details to arrange and carry out and there is the shock and sadness that has to be contained somehow. And then it is not our native place.

In our native place the whole extended family takes on so many duties and quietly every ritual and rite is completed. In this big city everything is more difficult. I am not sure what I would have done if this stranger had not entered our lives. But she did. She very quietly brought a kind of peace and orderliness to this city flat with its books which filled every space from the floor to the ceiling. She dealt with the books stacked under the beds and on the kitchen shelves and she didn't talk a great deal but listened very quietly to me and my son in this time of grieving.   —

I have not said anything about my son so I think this is the time to tell you a little about him. He would never speak about himself. He loved two things very much — music and books. Of course he had a regular job for many years, but his heart was not really in it. Whenever I met my relatives they would ask me only one question which seems to be the most important one asked in our country. "And when is your boy getting married? Do you not wish for grandchildren?" After my son was over thirty-five even this question stopped. He became what in western countries is called a confirmed bachelor. I did not mind. He was a good son and he cared for me. In this way our life had moved along — not happy but then not sad but in a normal regular pattern. Even if it was odd. Because we lived so far from our native place I did not have friends, but I pulled on. My daughter I have described earlier.

I will now use a somewhat sophisticated term that you will think is not the way I talk or even recount something — but I think most of us, specially those of us not really very articulate people, have secret ways we imagine we would speak if other people spoke to us more or asked for our opinion more or even just listened to our thoughts — the term is, though I might be a "footnote" in my family's life there is or rather was someone in mine, that is my life — who is now, was, the centre, so I will speak of him. In our culture a dog is not held very dear. In fact in my small hometown a dog was something you chased away as unclean or untouchable. Then maybe as a nuisance, then gradually as a watchdog to ward off bad things that came in the night or in the day — but not something ever to be part of a family or a friend. Think of nearly all the terms of abuse in our culture; they are usually ugly filthy words about a dog or a woman. But where a certain double standard or rather extreme hypocrisy pertains to women in our culture and how they are viewed, this does not happen with dogs. They are dirty, filthy, greedy, lusty, noisy, to be kicked and beaten always. They are not revered sometimes as gods or goddesses as mother, sisters and wives, they are bitches always and lousy sneaky bitches at all times. But in the big city far from my own small hometown one day on my way to somewhere there was a dog. This too is a rite of passage. I accept it. What else is there to do? My father would have said no that is not enough. It's the way you accept a thing that matters. What more do you want? Blood? Of course blood. Then it's not a punishment. All right. I accept it not as a punishment. As what, then? As retribution. The dog had cataract. Both his beautiful eyes. You can't do anything when a dog gets cataract. They ought to think of a way. He needs his eyes every bit as much, more really than a man does. Oh Golden Days had a way at the stairs once his eyes were really bad. A milky strange light or rather dimming of the light. Head sideways trying to find a chink — where the light might come through and he could get an idea where the corner of the step was so that he could get at the whole step. It could break the heart. The sight of Golden Days hesitating sometimes for nearly ten minutes before he thought he saw what clearly he could not see, and then trying his best. Down he'd go. With lopsided momentum, and land ignominiously on his bum. Then get up very fast looking around making sure no one had seen him.

Now this dog was my best friend. You have an idea now of my family. Or lack of family really. A husband who read all his life and mine and then died. A daughter who grew up and grew away and married a tall American boy and lived far away. Only a photograph to show that there was such a marriage. That I had, far away a son-in-law. And a son who was a quiet bachelor set in his ways, which were very private. And then my friend Golden Days. And then he died. But then this tall pale foreign girl in a sari and chappals took over my house. My son too, she took over. He stopped smoking. He never had a rum and coke. She helped him with his music. She saw to the house, to the quiet, to the details of the funeral. She replied to the condolence letters. She saw that I ate, that I went to bed. She helped me to bury Golden Days. And then she married my son. Her father came from England and from the airport he came straight to the wedding place. He was wearing a dark suit and she put a marigold into the lapel of his jacket and made him take off his shoes. It was a short ceremony but complete and it was very hot and I wish my husband and my daughter could have been there. We did not have an elaborate wedding feast but for the few friends who came it was an eccentric, unusual kind of wedding. Then the young couple went away to a nearby hill station for just a week. Her father went back to England.

And I went to my daughter in America — they invited me to come and stay with them for as long as I wanted. I said I would go for two weeks. And that is when everything happened. I should not have gone. One always feels that had one not done anything too out of the ordinary then life would have gone on in the same way. Before the two weeks were over I got a letter from my son telling me that my pale, tall daughter-in-law had died. She had got a rare kind of malaria and refused all medicines, and within the space of a week her father came back to India and was able to see her and embrace her for the last time. I returned to my home. It was even emptier than when I left. I had grown very fond of my unusual daughter-in-law and had hoped to have had many good and happy years with her. But it was not to be. My son retired into himself even more. We would meet very briefly for meals and then he would go to his room and play his music. He hardly spoke any more. So once again my life was very quiet. As quiet as my life in the cremation grounds after my death. Whenever I feel excessively sorry for my life I think of that poor father who had come so trustingly to the marriage of his only child in a strange land. Had journeyed long hours in an aeroplane wearing his best suit. Had accepted strange wedding rituals, worn no shoes, had worn a bright Indian marigold in the lapel of his jacket. And had come back again for her funeral rituals. I wonder why we become parents. When he was leaving he said to me, "Was it for this the clay grew tall?"

19   *Elvira's Priest*

At eighteen I went with my husband to live where he worked. Angola. I lived there for thirty years without once coming back to my home in Goa. My mother visited once during all those years and my father twice. It was in those days rather a long journey. We had no children. My husband must have been fond of me because he never sought to marry again or as far as I know never had a mistress. Its true that these things are usually found out when somebody dies. Life was good, said everybody, in Angola, so I am repeating what I kept hearing. I looked after a large house, I read a great deal and I walked a lot. I never made any real friends. Nobody made friends with the blacks and I didn't much care for our own type of person. On some of my long walks I did look at the homes and at the faces of the people we didn't invite to our homes and I was much ashamed but there was little I could do about it. And the years passed and I kept a great secret in my heart. Mostly I look into a place of shadows and darkness. I longed for my village in Goa and for our great house that overlooked a large, green, paddy field. My husband was good to me and I never told him about my longings. What could he do about them? It was not his fault after all. I was to blame because I had not been faithful to him. I had been unfaithful from the day we were married.

And then one day he died. After the funeral I packed up everything, all the years I packed into trunks and crates and came home.

Mama and Papa were both dead and there was only old Lourdhina and somebody to look after the garden. But it was wonderful to be home again, almost not quite as it had been all those years ago. Some old people called, people who had known my parents and came to see me, courtesy calls. I offered them a glass of port and cake and they soon went away. I was close to fifty years old, a widow. But I had come home.

I avoided the small room that led into the large dining room but finally had to face it. It was a cream-walled room and had a delicate, most unusual for Goa, painting running across a whole wall, of white birds and green fields and a woman waiting. This was the room in which I had first met "my love, my dove, my undefiled one". For eighteen years I had not met anyone "like him", not a male cousin or visiting friends with their growing or grown-up sons. Not one had affected me in the slightest. And then on my eighteenth birthday which was also my wedding day I met my love. Since he did not say anything, how could I speak? I was too young, such a thing had never happened to me before. My uncle introduced him to my mother and then my father and then to me. I looked into the palest grey eyes and they looked at me and that was my undoing. I have never felt as I felt in that moment and perhaps never will again. He was the new young priest come to our parish and one of his first duties was to be this morning assisting our old family priest at my wedding. So that was that. But it was not really, because I could not bear what was happening. I felt surely something would happen. My wedding would not happen. This man would not allow it. He would speak. I looked at my mother, I felt she might guess, my father would say something. The man I was to marry, would not marry me. But nothing happened. I said, "Mama, I cannot, I cannot, listen to me Mama." She thinking I was nervous, overwrought, said, "Be calm, do not worry, don't cry, don't cry."

That day eighty people dined in the great dining room. Nobody who was there ever forgot that dinner. Little boys of ten, now decades later, remembered that feast.

Everybody talked of how many chickens were slaughtered, how many piglings lost their lives, how many almonds were peeled, how many garrafaons of wine were brought up out of the cellar. I looked lovely. Cream coloured lace from Portugal. I wept bitterly, "She is young, she is sad because she will have to leave Goa, leave her Mama and Papa."

I knew why I wept so bitterly. I wanted that young man. I knew he was a priest. I wanted him and I wanted him to want me. He came to the wedding feast. I spoke to him of this and that. And then I said, "I am going far away, did you know?" I said, "Will you wait, wait for me?"

He said, "I will wait."

I said, "However long it takes?"

He said, "I will wait, however long it takes."

I said, "Promise me."

He said, "I promise."

In this way I was unfaithful to my husband from the

day of my wedding. I have recounted the next thirty years of my life. Till my husband died.

I went to our village church the very first Sunday I returned. I went alone and I went for him. The church was very full, it being Easter. I thought "If he is here he will touch my hair when he blesses me. I shall die if he does not touch me." Many faces she recognized but they were all turned so much older. I have grown older. He will think of me as I was on my wedding day. And now he will see this older woman. Past her prime. I saw the Easter lilies in their pots of red earth. She hoped he would touch her head in blessing, in recognition. She touched her head to feel or try to feel what he would feel when he did. If he did. Touch her. She thought of Peter Abelard, and the Sin of Father Amaro and she thought of the unfairness of it all. She thought, "Let him be here. Let him touch me." Though there was much grey in her hair, it was still soft.

When he came she did not see him. She saw his pale grey eyes. She saw his grey hair. She did not know what he said in that sermon. She kept hearing "Wait for me, however long it takes. Promise me." He had kept his promise.

He was alive. He had waited. "Promise me."

She went back to the big house and waited thinking of that long-ago morning. Her wedding day. She had woken early and gone straight to the window. She had looked at what had been there for eighteen years of her life. First the garden, then the wall, then the road, then the vast green paddy field and beyond it the groves of palm and mango and betel. She looked again and this time she saw first the palm then the paddy field, then the road and then the garden and then a knock at her door, and her Mama came in saying, "Today is a very good day, I have prayed and I know today is blessed. You must get ready." And, "Yes mama" she had said and gone to get ready for her wedding.

And now as she waited she thought of how long she had waited and would not wait any longer. When he came to her finally he said, "You have, Elvira, known much in your life, you have seen much. But I have waited a long while."

"I have also missed much," she said, "I have missed my whole life. Till now." Of course they had to move away to another place for a while but then they returned to where it had all begun. They had the much-loved house and garden and the paddy field and the groves of palm beyond. And sometimes from their window, as they watched, a white bird would suddenly leave the green and climb into the blue.

20 *Ithaka*

A bee buzzed in the warm almost hot afternoon as we lingered over tea thinking about Tess and Hardy and what miles and miles his heroine walked and agonized about her love and her fate. All morning they had trudged Hardy's landscape and thought about Stonehenge and its scale. How in photographs and in writing it had always seemed immense and how in actual fact the stones were so much smaller though still giving out an atmosphere of grey loneliness and mystery. Josie handed around brown bread and butter and "honey", she said, "or my own jam? Megan should be with us soon. She is so anxious to meet you." In a short while she did and went straight to a pram stationed near a Japonica bush. She peered in and then lifted out her sister calling out, "Felicity" and swung her round and round. After a while she joined us. A lovely girl as sometimes the unspoilt English girl can be. Fresh and intelligent, talking of this and that and recounting how some men outside the village pub had called out " 'Here comes the cream!' Because I don't live here and come up from London," she explained. After her tea she said she'd show us around their village; she loved it and was proud of it.

We finally entered the little church, dark and cool and very quiet, "Lots of our ancestors are buried here; it's been our church for a long while. I do love the sense of continuity but sometimes I do want to get away. I plan to go to India next year, I want to trek, to see mountains, to see temples." I told her how different our temples were compared to churches and cathedrals, how much my husband and I loved the cool quiet of old cathedrals, stained glass windows compared to the noise and crowding and bustle of our temples. All the activity. The flowers and the incense and the holiday atmosphere. "I'd love to see your temples," she said again. I told her I hoped she would come and soon.

Long after we got back to India we got a letter from Josie telling us that Megan was coming out and would we please help her set her off on her journey. She arrived the following weekend and we took her home and sat in our Delhi garden with maps spread out on the grass helping her decide her route. Since she wanted walking and climbing and temples we helped her decide on the Kumaon hills and talked of what little we had seen hoping always that we would go back. So that is how it was.

One early morning we saw her off on the first leg of her journey. A slip of a girl with honey coloured hair, worn long. A postcard from Almora told us she had a great journey up, even stopped at Corbett Park and missed the bus and so had started her walk from there to Ranikhet. We never heard from her again but often wondered how she was faring. Did I mention she had honey-coloured hair, worn long? The last time we saw her was getting on a bus, a small figure with rather a large blue backpack and sleeping bag. She had borrowed a couple of my William books — "for when I get gloomy", she had said. Oh yes, her postcard mentioned she hadn't touched dear William — she was always so exhausted by eventide. We did think of her off and on during the next year but realized she must have returned home. "With my two William books," I thought bitterly. "Anyway I'm sure they are safe."

We then got a Christmas card with a little message about how Felicity was now all over the place and then something oddly chilling. "We have heard nothing from Megan. This troubles us greatly. Her last postcard ever so long ago from Almora said she had visited the temples at Jageshwar and Chittai. She could stay forever, she said, it was that beautiful.

"If we don't hear from her early in the new year we plan to come out. We are hoping that perhaps you might have heard from her. Have you?" I wrote immediately of course feeling oddly troubled — "but there can't be anything the matter it must be just the post," I wrote to Josie. At the end of January another short note from Josie which said, "We are heartsick filled with fear and sadness. Will contact you as soon as we arrive." In the meantime we contacted the British Embassy and all our contacts to see if there was anything they might know that might help in trying to find Megan. Something, anything, soon, before her parents arrived. It all drew a blank. No English girl was reported as missing, no one in the hospitals in that area. That sort of thing. Perhaps that was good news. When Josie and her husband Jake arrived, they looked anxious but eager to start their search immediately. We saw them off on their journey, the first lap of which they were to do in a rather battered taxi with a congenial driver. It was the same spot from where the small figure of Megan had boarded a bus so many months ago. From

Delhi they drove to Corbett Park which was to be their first stop as it had been Megan's. They passed broken trucks and the debris of horrendous accidents but their driver was a cheerful sort and said he would get them there safely. They held each other's hands all the way as they passed huge trucks, cycles, string cots under dusty trees, cows with three legs dragging a fourth, and fifty stray, thin, mad-looking dogs. At Corbett Park they stopped and looked at the guesthouse register and there was Megan's familiar signature and a scribbled entry about, "not seeing any wild life, alas! But much silence broken by bird sounds."

They felt curiously close to her after that and by late evening climbed to Ranikhet and stopped at an old English hotel. It was charming with wood floors and a garden and the brass shone. After hot baths they went to the empty dining room and had a four-course English meal ending with a superb caramel custard and met the manager. They asked him if they could see the hotel register of rather a long time ago and he remembered their daughter and said she had stayed in the same room as they had now, how they had had a wonderful chat. She had told him this stay would be her last luxury, from now on she would be sleeping just anywhere she had said. They asked him if he knew about her whereabouts. He looked perplexed for a longish while and then said, "You do not know where she is? You are her parents and this you do not know? She said she was walking to Almora and beyond. I asked her to stay with us on her return journey, after that nothing!" They looked at the register and found her dear signature and a note on the "yummy food — especially the caramel custard."

That night they went dejected to bed and watched the fire dance on the ceiling and thought of Megan sleeping in this bed looking up at the ceiling, thinking her thoughts. Now they thought theirs and prayed, "Dear God let her be all right, look after her if she needs your help in any way." Next morning they set off. Walking like Megan. With a packed lunch and the many good wishes of the manager.

They walked very well that first day. They looked around as they walked. There was still forest land but there had been much indiscriminate cutting down of healthy looking trees. They were greatly cheered when late afternoon they met two backpackers who were going to stop the night at a place called Mirtola. There was an ashram and if they had the space they were hoping they would be able to stay the night there. Josie and her husband Jake thanked them and said they might try too. They walked together and the two trekkers said they were "checking out" these hills and hopefully, next year the Himalayas!

They reached Mirtola and found since one of the cottages was empty, the four of them were welcome to stay. That night Josie wept bitterly but very quietly. "I can feel Megan close by, very close." She said this over and over. "I miss her, how much I miss her. We have to find her. Do you think we will?"

"Don't cry, don't, its just the first day you are tired, don't be disheartened. Tomorrow you'll feel different, you'll see. I promise. Sleep now." Jake comforted. Indeed the new morning felt very good, the air cold but smelling so good. A very tall man in dark red robes and a large dog wished them well on their journey and held Josie's hand a fraction and seemed to look deep into her eyes. They looked back once and found him still standing there. He had not moved. They walked. And they walked and by lunch time found themselves near a stream, cold and fresh. They checked their maps. Next day they should be in Binsar and Josie said, "Binsar keeps making me think of that Yeats poem, no not Yeats it was Hopkins, remember, 'Binsey poplars,' not Binsar. 'All felled, felled are all felled. O if we but knew what we do. When we delve or hew-hack and rack the growing green' — Will we find her? Does she want us to find her? Am I going mad? I feel so dislocated!"

"Of course you are not going mad and of course you feel dislocated. We have come from a far-off place to a far-off place, and we are looking for Megan as we used to look for her when she was little. Remember how she would hide, and once we looked and looked and found her in the old church and how she said, 'I knew you would find me, that's why I hid, you must always find me,' " said Jake.

They trudged on. In the evening they found some circular cottages and a friendly gregarious man who owned them. As he unlocked their door he said "Look at this bush, when it is dark, as the last rays of the sun go down. You will see a fine and beautiful miracle." And so they did. As the sun set and died little yellow buds opened and the air grew fragrant around them. And the man said, "The name is Nisha, when daylight goes they open, so think of them when you fear darkness or despair." They felt curiously sustained.

Next day they trekked through pine and birch and joined a group of devotees going to the temple of Chittai and they walked with them thinking Megan must have done this. She wanted to go to all the temples in this region. Their guidebook told them that this was the temple where your wishes could come true. There were little bells hung everywhere in the temple and outside. Josie and Jake bought two bells just to be on the safe side and hung them on a tree outside and wished with their eyes closed, as in a fairy tale. They wished only to see their daughter Megan — that is all. It was a humble wish. And then they left.

Often they would ask travellers if they had seen their daughter, "small with a blue back-pack and long honey coloured hair". Most people said no and that there were so many foreigners during the season, why not ask at all the houses that took in trekkers. They did ask, they asked all the time, and they looked carefully whenever they saw groups of trekkers. And their hearts skipped a beat whenever they saw a blue backpack.

After a few days they walked to another famous temple called Jageshwar. It was very beautiful, set among trees and almost hidden from view. They wished they were seeing it as tourists, they wished they were seeing this temple with Megan. That night they slept in their sleeping bags and thought of Megan seeing the temple, of Megan looking at the great mountain peaks, of Megan trekking alone. They looked up at the stars and prayed that Megan was trekking with a companion. That Megan was not alone. Perhaps when Megan had seen the great mountain peaks she had thought all else is commonplace and had decided to live where she could see them everyday. They did feel her presence. Here, strongly. She was here. But where? One terrible night Josie dreamed that they had found Megan. She was skin and bone. The little blue and white Della Robia medallion was still around her neck and all over her arms and legs there were the cruel marks of needles. Josie cried and cried in her dream and said, "We heve found her, found her, why are we crying?" Jake decided they were going back and soon. Josie would collapse if this went on much longer. "We must go back — remember there is Felicity. She must miss us. She is so little. Also I know now that Megan will find her way back to us or she has found her peace. We are going back. The time is not ripe. She is not ready." That was a long speech for Jake to have made and it comforted Josie.

After many months we in Delhi got a letter from Josie. The letter asked us when we might be going back to the hills. They would like us to go to Chitthai temple for them and tie two little bells for them. They had asked a boon and had not fulfilled a promise they had made.

Josie one afternoon playing with Felicity near the Japonica bush thought she heard a voice which was of course Megan's saying, "Ma, try to understand. Now I am here, please Ma."

"But what about us Megan, what about us? Don't we count anymore?"

"Of course you do, more than you can ever know. Much more."

"Then why, why Megan why must we be so unhappy? You don't know how your father suffers and he can't howl and cry like I do. And Felicity, she asks and asks — what is it all for, when will you come back to us?"

"Ma, I was with you when you came, I even saw you — if ever I died it was that morning. You even turned back once. I was there. If I had come running after you that morning I would never have finished my journey. I was not yet strong. Please try and understand. Here I can see Trishul and Nandakhot, on a clear day I can see all the peaks with snow on them."

"But Megan, I am a mother, your mother, I want to touch you, to hug you, to tuck you into bed. This is what I want to do. It is not much. But it is everything to me."

"Ma, do you remember the book of poems you gave me when I was twenty-one? One poem you had marked and underlined and I know it was your most favourite one. My journey was true, not ever merely to run away from you my most perfect family, remember, 'Ithaka has given you your lovely journey. Without Ithaka you would not have set out.'

'Ithaka has no more to give you now.' Remember the lines and what they mean. I do. Now."

21 Desperately Seeking Suzanne

The first time I met her was at the beginning of term. Newnham 1953. I was a frightened nineteen year old off a P&O boat from Bombay. I was moving into the cottage called Whitstead in the grounds of the college. It had eight rooms for eight students doing their degrees in two years instead of three. I was enormously afraid. There was a dear housekeeper called Mrs. Milne and there was Suzanne. Most of the young women had been in the cottage for a year so they knew everything – I had to learn everything. I was new. I was stupid and I didn't know why I was there.

She was very tall with short curly auburny hair wearing cords and a jacket, a brown suede jacket and she was just about to leave for work at the library. But she came back and talked to me and showed me where everything was and then took me to her room for a cup of coffee. She looked marvellous, like nothing I had seen before and so easy and natural and friendly. "An Aussie", she said. Her accent I got used to almost immediately. She helped me to move into the smallest room, warm and on the ground floor with a large bay window looking out onto the garden. She helped me arrange my books and to rent a radio, helped me to rent a cycle and a second-hand gown and my first large pullover from a men's shop and a pair of trousers – "now you'll be warm" she said. She was practical and helpful and such a good friend to me. She trudged through rain and snow with me when I was home-sick and blue, jogged me along when dreaded Anglo-saxon baffled and beat me. Late night coffee or cocoa, talking of geology, her subject and English Literature which was mine. We'd sit on her carpet close to the gas fire and all around there would be a sea of papers, notes in her fine handwriting with wonderful meticulously drawn sketches of just about everything. "I'm writing to my parents, to my brother I write a weekly letter." I thought how wonderful to get letters like that. She was an artist really. Except she didn't know it. She wanted to fly - when she got back, she planned to learn, "then I can see what my country is really like," she said. "There is no other way to get around it, and learn it. All those vast spaces.

It's too big for cars or trains. You come to Podders, we'll check out the scene together." Easter break we travelled third class to a little town up in the Pyrenees. Filthy rain and cold, very cold but Suzanne tramped around taking photographs of grave-stones and wild flowers and odd little cottages and their inmates and on our last day the sun came out and Suzanne went to sleep in a field of sheep and a single cow came to look at her. That photograph I took. I have it still.

Suzanne used to work late into the night when the cottage was very quiet but she was always welcoming if I climbed the stairs to her room - unable to sleep, worrying or anxious she would push aside her papers and say, "now what wee one?" We would talk and talk, she said she would come to India to look me up among other things like the Taj Mahal and the Himalayas. I said I would get to Aussie land and we'd raise a glass. I only knew her a year but it felt forever there was so much that year. King's college chapel from even song and secondhand books on Saturdays at Davids and just walking and walking. Learning to punt. And then it was time for her to go back. The sun shone brilliantly for her farewell party in our garden at Whitstead. We wore bright saris and the flowers were all out and Suzanne wore a skirt for a change and we all sang songs and we toasted her all of us Christopher and Shaila and Ruth and David and Jaques and Maggie and Sylvo and Mrs. Milne. Late that night I cried and cried knowing that a phase was over, certain things would never happen again. I was never going to see Sue again. Sue said, "rubbish, You'll not get rid of me so easily – stop crying Podders or I can't get to bed."

And the next day she left.

I had another whole year. Someone else moved into her room, someone else's dressing gown hung on the bathroom door. I missed her enormously. I resented everyone new who came to Whitstead. I missed her tall graceful frame, her stride as she walked, her practical common sense, her jokes, her laughter, her sketches, her brown suede jacket with a belt – our later night chats. I missed her. Her letters started coming; never flimsy air-letters, always fat envelopes, very thin paper and lots of drawings and news and plans. She was teaching already and hoped I was not "glooming and listening to Mahler and those dead infants." She was working hard and already learning to fly three evenings a week. And what was I doing, she wrote. There would be her marvellous sketches of me in a huge pullover, hair in a bun gazing at a wax swan's head on my window sill. Neglecting a tutorial I was supposed to be doing. "No glooming mind - if it becomes too serious then off you go to Napwell Wood and pick lots of flowers for both of us." She had the gift of life and joy, more than anyone I could ever meet in my life.

When my Cambridge days were over she still wrote to me and I still wrote to her and her fat letter packets would bring such great hours of sharing and reminiscing. Her letters helped me in all the months of adjusting and looking for a job and the heat and dust and missing Cambridge and its ways. Often as we raised a toast on a birthday or a wedding anniversary, I would say as Suzanne had done as we drank cider or mead. "I looks at you and I raises my glass."

After a long while and I'm talking years now, I stopped writing. To my eternal shame, Suzanne did not stop for ages after that. She seemed to understand some of the things that were happening to me. She seemed to know and understand. My life had nothing happening in it that was letter-worthy and then I kept getting ill and sad and then I became lazy. I was a bad friend for a long while. In all that time she was still teaching and researching in her field and she had not only a licence but her own little plane to fly. She wrote about the outbacks and vast expanses of desert and scrub and rock. She drew many sketches of herself in old fashioned flying goggles waving out of her plane, shades of *Out of Africa*. She talked of Sidney Nolan's paintings, she talked of Patrick White and I remained silent. She wrote of coming to India, asked me when I was coming "Aussiewards". "Time for a chat Podders, a long chat" she wrote. It was indeed time for a chat. Suddenly, magically she wrote of coming to Kathmandu. She was going trekking. Letters crossed and checked and dates fixed for meeting on her way in and on her way out.

But my mother died. Suddenly she died and I went home. And that was very much that. A terrible time. A time that went on and on. So I missed Suzanne. She wrote saying, "Not to worry, we'll check out the scene N.P. Not to worry."

Another twenty years passed. And another bit of magic. I was to go with my father to Fiji and we had a day on the way out and a day on the way back. I wrote frantically and with dates and the address of the hotel everything. When I got to Sydney I rang her number in Melbourne and the woman said, "Dr. Duigan does not live here any more. Hasn't lived here for the last five years." I rang the University and her department and got the same answer. I rang every Duigan in the book. I had no response. I left feeling desperate and sad. I left Australia thinking so now this has happened. This is it. Why did this have to happen? Where was she? We could have met and I could have held her large firm hand with its long fingers and raised a glass. So near and yet so far and all the other ironic cliches. What a lot of stuff to talk about. What did she look like, was she as white-haired as I was forty years on. There was all of Patrick White to talk about, art galleries to visit, a ride in her plane to Ayers Rock and perhaps to that strange place in Picnic at Hanging Rock to hear the pan pipes playing. Talked and walked and reminisced. Where was Suzanne? On the lonely plane back I thought. Well, it's just as well - maybe it was too long to expect, to still like each other, still find things to talk about and laugh about. Maybe she didn't smoke anymore. Maybe we'd loathe the sight of each other - it had been known to happen after all - still. We were in our twenties then and now we were well into our sixties. Life was not a story book with a happy ending the last shot in a film walking into the sunset or the sunrise. Cut.

Sadly I re-read Voss, and *Tree of Man* and *Riders in a Chariot* and thought of Suzanne. I thought of Suzanne in each of these books and Suzanne's plane crashing in a lonely remote spot being helped by Abo's and living with them. I thought of her legs crushed under the wings of her aeroplane. I thought of Suzanne without water wandering in the outbacks out of her mind with pain and lack of food and water, wearing a torn brown suede jacket - with a belt. These nightmares went on for a long while and then I got a letter from Australia. A letter from Suzanne's nephew saying that Soo had died six months ago of cancer. So the thing that I had not allowed myself even to think of had happened. Suzanne, the strong Suzanne, the brave and quick with life Suzanne, striding to Grantchester or asleep in a field in the Pyrenees with a cow looking at her. Suzanne helping with the blues, helping with hundreds of cups of coffee and cigarettes. Suzanne was dead now and I hadn't been with her to help her. It's wrong to think you meet people again once a phase is over. It's wrong to think love or loyalty or friendship means you'll meet again. I'll never believe all that crap again. I had sought Suzanne and not found her to tell her I had looked and looked for her.

Now as I watch the Magregor Saga, the man from Snowy River or even The Flying Doctors, I see Suzanne in her plane flying over vast lands of rock and desert and sheepland and gorges or long ago rivers and I see her land her plane and building a small fire and boil a billy can of coffee. I see her reading and sketching stretched out on the ground. I think of her a lot. I hope she didn't suffer too much. I hope she fought the big C. I can hear her big laugh and see her walking in her cords and her belted suede jacket. She was invincible. I had thought she would live forever. Or at least till we had met again.